HANG HIM HIGH

Center Point
Large Print

Also by Lewis B. Patten and available from
Center Point Large Print:

Shadow of the Gun
Cañon Creek
Gun This Man Down
Giant on Horseback

**This Large Print Book carries the
Seal of Approval of N.A.V.H.**

HANG HIM HIGH

A WESTERN DUO

Lewis B. Patten

CENTER POINT LARGE PRINT
THORNDIKE, MAINE

This Center Point Large Print edition
is published in the year 2018 by arrangement with
Golden West Literary Agency.

The text of this Large Print edition is unabridged.
In other aspects, this book may vary
from the original edition.
Printed in the United States of America
on permanent paper.
Set in 16-point Times New Roman type.

ISBN: 978-1-68324-660-2 (hardcover)
ISBN: 978-1-68324-664-0 (paperback)

Library of Congress Cataloging-in-Publication Data

Names: Patten, Lewis B., author.
Title: Hang him high : a western duo / Lewis B. Patten.
Description: Center Point Large Print edition. | Thorndike, Maine :
    Center Point Large Print, 2018.
Identifiers: LCCN 2017045627| ISBN 9781683246602
    (hardcover : alk. paper) | ISBN 9781683246640 (pbk. : alk. paper)
Subjects: LCSH: Large type books. | GSAFD: Western stories.
Classification: LCC PS3566.A79 D34 2018 | DDC 813/.54—dc22
LC record available at https://lccn.loc.gov/2017045627

TABLE OF CONTENTS

Dance-Hall Gal

I

The crowd stood silently, stunned. Heat beat down on the dusty street, forming a pool between the two rows of false-fronted buildings. The auctioneer poured a glassful of tepid water and drank it. His face, what could be seen of it around his black beard, was brick-red. He mopped his streaming brow.

Beside the auctioneer stood Will Geier, the banker, cool, amused, triumphant. Something inside the young rancher, Tom Otis, welled up so strongly that he pushed through the crowd toward the auctioneer's raised platform. The crowd made way for him. He went up the two steps and stopped before Will Geier.

What does a man say to another who has just stolen the best ranch in the country from him? What does he say when he holds only a busted flush and the other man a handful of aces? There was nothing much Tom Otis could say. But there was one thing he could do.

He said: "Geier, get your hands up! I'm going to beat you to a pulp!"

His words were clear, and they halted the crowd that turned, watching. Geier took a step away, and Tom Otis's left whistled through thin air close to the banker's head. But Tom's right, following through, made a sodden, solid crack against Geier's jaw. Geier fell back, tripped on the edge of the platform, and sprawled into the street, yelling: "Sheriff! Sheriff!"

Tom was after him, running. An outstretched foot tripped him, and he sprawled on top of Geier. His hands were reaching for Geier's throat when a gun muzzle dug savagely against his ribs, and a wild voice yelled: "Get off him! Damn you, get off him!"

Tom Otis came to his feet. Geier, surging up full of rage, swung a left and right into Tom's face, driving him back again to the platform. Sheriff Yarbo held a gun on Tom, yelling: "Let him alone, or by hell I'll kill you!"

A certain decisiveness in the lawman's voice told Tom he really would. Tom came to his feet, debating between Yarbo and Geier. A couple of men from the crowd seized Geier's arms. Then Lily Street, from the Colorado Saloon, stepped between Tom and the sheriff deliberately.

Yarbo spoke from behind her: "Get out of town, Otis! Get out and stay out!"

The wildness in Tom Otis urged him to take Yarbo, take Geier, take the whole town, now while the mood was on him. Instead, he whirled and broke back through the crowd, hurrying his steps. He had to get away—had to, before he lost what little judgment remained to him.

He heard Lily call his name, but he did not

slow his swiftly striding pace. Sympathy was one thing he couldn't stand right now. He heard her running behind him, and curbed his impulse for further speed. He'd been robbed blind today. He'd been robbed and he'd stood and taken it. But he would not let the town see him running from a woman.

He turned to face her. His face was white, even in this heat. He was a big man, lean as whang leather and almost as brown. His hair was yellow, his eyes an odd shade of blue—a light blue. Eyes that caught the attention and held it. Right now, they were like two blue marbles, cold and hard.

Behind Lily he could see the crowd beginning to break up. Forming into small groups, they gave vent to their indignation in low whispers, whispers that died as Will Geier put his red-eyed, furious gaze upon them. The banker stuffed a bunch of papers into a leather briefcase and, with a short nod to the auctioneer, strode toward the bank.

There was sympathy in Lily Street's brown eyes, but she had the good sense not to mention it. She said: "Well, that's over. What will you do now, Tom?"

He shrugged, and his hard-planed face settled into lines of bitterness. "I know what I want to do, and, if I don't get out of town, I'm likely to do it."

She said: "Will you wait until I can change my clothes? I want to talk to you."

Refusal was on the tip of his tongue. Lily touched his arm. Her hand was soft, but her grip was firm. "Please, Tom."

He shrugged. "All right. Hurry up."

Lily ran lightly across the street and into the hotel. Tom looked downstreet. The crowd was spreading out, some of the men coming toward him. With anger and frustration boiling in him he crossed the street and stood in the shade of the hotel. Fishing in his shirt pocket he withdrew a sack of tobacco and rolled a cigarette with shaking fingers.

Impatiently he turned and stared through the hotel window. There was the handbill, pasted against the inside of the window.

AUCTION!

Below that in smaller letters was the announcement:

> August 27th. The Anchor Ranch will be auctioned to the highest bidder. 27,000 acres deeded, 64,000 acres in state leases. To satisfy mortgage held by the Union Bank of Adams City, Colorado.

There was some small print at the bottom of the sheet, listing livestock and equipment. Tom didn't read that.

And now the auction was over. Tom Otis looked north, away from the river. Everywhere he saw the rims, the towering, massive borders of rimrock that marked the boundaries of Anchor range. No one could look north out of Adams City without looking at Anchor. Now it belonged to Will Geier—to Banker Geier who had stolen it legally for less than a quarter of its value. And Tom Otis himself was a drifter, without even a job. A gun and a small handful of silver coins. That was all he had left to show for having owned Anchor Ranch.

Anger was like a core of glowing coals in his brain. Anger because of the way this had been done. A couple of men approached him, seemed about to speak, but his scowl drove them away, made them veer off toward the open doors of the saloon.

The stableman came around the hotel from the stable at the rear, leading Lily Street's dainty chestnut gelding. Tom Otis took the reins. Lily came out of the hotel, and he helped her up into the side-saddle. Lily wore a straight riding skirt and a checkered shirt-waist that was like a man's shirt. Her gleaming dark hair was piled up atop her head. She was pale. Tom mounted and followed her north along Main to the edge of town.

Neither spoke until they cleared the limits of the town. Tom, as though realizing that he was

13

riding by habit toward Anchor, veered away from the road, heading around town toward the river. This was the town dump, littered with scrap lumber, old plaster, tin cans, and bottles. The horses picked their way daintily through the rubble.

Lily asked: "What was it you wanted to do in town, Tom?"

His laugh was harsh. "Don't be a fool, Lily. I wanted to kill Will Geier. Maybe I'll do it yet."

Lily remained silent.

At the edge of the dump, something bright orange in the bottom of a shallow wash caught Tom's eye. His glance flicked away, darted back involuntarily. Something about that color was familiar. He had ridden almost past when a breeze stirred, stirred the orange something at the bottom of that wash. He reined aside, looking down.

What rage he had felt before was puny compared to the fury that tore through him now like a holocaust. But his voice was still, tight.

"Lily. Come here."

Her horse ranged up beside his. She looked down. She said: "Tom! Oh, no!"

Tom swung to the ground, climbed down into the wash. When he came back out, he held a handful of paper handbills, only a part of the bunch that lay in the bottom of the wash.

He said: "This is why there were no big out-of-town crowds in town today. This is why there weren't any bids besides Will Geier's."

The handbills announcing the sale were supposed to have gone upriver to all the towns for a hundred miles, and downriver as far as Moab, Utah. If they'd gone where they'd been supposed to go, there'd have been a dozen bidders for Anchor, bidders who knew the worth of Anchor's lush grass and fat cattle, and who had the cash to back their bids. If these handbills had gone out as they were supposed to, Tom Otis would be richer this afternoon by $40,000 or $50,000, maybe more.

He said: "I thought Geier was rushing this auction. Now I know why. He didn't want word of the auction to get noised around by word of mouth."

Still holding the handbills, he swung to saddle. His mouth was a thin, straight line. There was murder in his eyes. Their lids narrowed dangerously. He reined his horse around, leaned forward preparatory to touching spurs to the animal's sides. Lily Street's voice was almost a scream: "Tom! Wait!"

He looked at her. She rode over and caught his horse's head. Fright stared at him out of her eyes. Her lips were bloodless.

She cried: "Tom, I don't blame you! I don't blame you for wanting to kill him. But what will it get you? Everybody knows how you feel, but

15

killing him is no solution. It won't get Anchor back for you. You'll go to jail and they'll hang you. Geier's no saddle bum you can kill in a fight. Tom, please!"

His face didn't relax, but the resolution drained out of him. She was right, of course. Will Geier was a big man in western Colorado. A moneyed man, one with a lot of political influence. Tom's voice held the essence of bitterness: "So I just forget about these? So I just sit back and let him steal Anchor?"

"I don't know. Oh, Tom, I don't know. But don't do anything today. Promise me that. Promise me you won't do anything today."

Tom Otis felt like a man who has been struck by a rattlesnake, then asked to spare the snake. He could feel tightness building up in his nerves, pressure on the increase in his tortured brain. Too many things had happened in the past two weeks.

First, his father, old Bob, had been thrown, and dragged to death on the way to town. As though that were not enough, Geier had immediately demanded payment on Bob Otis's note, already overdue.

Tom had started a cattle roundup, but Geier had stopped it. A roundup and drive, he'd said, would take a month and a half. He couldn't wait that long. His bank, he'd claimed, was in serious financial difficulties. The bank had notes of its

16

own to meet. He'd said he had planned to borrow what he needed from a Denver bank, using the Anchor mortgage as security, but with old Bob gone Anchor had become a bad risk for a bank three hundred miles away. He'd been regretful, but behind that mask of regret and reluctance Tom had sensed Geier's smiling triumph.

Maybe eventually Tom could have reconciled himself to losing Anchor. But he would never reconcile himself to this—this stealing Anchor for a $10,000 mortgage simply because it had been rigged so that no competing bidders had been present.

Also, Geier's story that he was desperate for cash was now proved a lie. For if his story had been true, he would not have been interested in bidding on Anchor himself. Tom was slowly being forced to the conclusion that it had been a steal from the beginning. A carefully engineered steal.

He growled savagely: "I'll get it back. I'll never quit until I've got it back."

Lily was insistent, pleading: "Tom, think it out before you do anything. Please, Tom!"

He nodded shortly, reluctantly. "All right."

He turned in his saddle and stuffed the handful of handbills into his saddlebags.

Lily reined her horse toward the, river, not looking back. After hesitating a moment, Tom followed.

The sun was like a hot iron against his neck. Heat waves rose shimmeringly from the gray-green sagebrush that covered the land. The river was a broad, sluggish ribbon of muddy brown.

Lily dismounted in the shade of a giant cottonwood and dropped her reins. Her horse wandered off and began to crop grass. She looked up at Tom, her eyes telling him nothing of her feelings, her desires. She sank down on the ground, bracing herself with her hands behind her. Tom glowered out at the sluggish river.

Lily said—"Sit down, Tom."—and he turned to look at her.

She was a small girl. Standing, she came just to the hollow of Tom's throat, but her body was fully rounded. Just now, the top button of her tight shirt-waist came unbuttoned and he could see the full, lush ripeness of her breasts. She had brown eyes, dark hair, skin that was white and smooth and unblemished. The eyes were wise, too, much too wise for her years. She knew men and what it was that drove them. Though Tom could not know it, right now she was thinking of one thing that drove men, that could make them forget.

She said again—"Sit down, Tom."—and he sank down beside her. She hitched herself closer to him, until one of her thighs touched his.

Something stirred in him besides the anger.

Her fragrance was sweet. She put her small hand on Tom's arm and he understood that she was offering him something.

Swiftly he turned. His arms closed about her. Her own arms went about him, and she fell back. Tom put his lips down savagely against her, hungrily.

There was neither hesitation nor retreat in Lily. Burning fire ran in Tom Otis's veins. He drew away, breathing fast. Lily had always been friendly toward Tom, but this was the first time she had shown any special interest in him. He knew a nagging suspicion.

He asked harshly: "What was that for?"

Lily's eyes were cool. She said: "Maybe I thought you'd had enough taken from you today. Maybe I wanted to give you something. But you spoiled it." She didn't meet his eyes.

Before he could stop her, she sprang to her feet. Lightly she ran to her horse, as lightly mounted to her saddle.

Tom said: "Wait a minute!"

He tried to catch the bridle of her horse, but she whirled the animal around and drummed her heels against his side. She left Tom staring after her, his heart thumping wildly. He scowled and cursed. He kicked a rock and hurt his toe.

For the first time today, a light grin twisted his long mouth. Yet his eyes were puzzled. Perhaps her reason for wanting to had been sympathy for him. But she wanted something from him, too. Of that he was sure.

He mounted and rode back toward town.

II

Riding slowly, Tom Otis came back into Adams City. Lily's actions had puzzled him, but she had stirred him as well. He was no different from other men in the country, and they all wanted Lily. It was hard for Tom to put out of his mind the incontrovertible fact that she had offered herself to him. Why? Because she felt sorry for him? A consolation prize?

He laughed, and the laugh was not pleasant.

He dismounted before the Ringold Dry Goods Store and looped his reins about the rail. As he climbed to the shady walk, he was conscious that the sun was sinking fast in the west. He went past Ringold's and mounted the outside staircase that led up to Phil Wickware's office.

Wickware was Adams City's only lawyer. He was a friend of Geier's, but he had also been a friend of old Bob Otis's.

His office door was open. Tom stepped off the high landing and into the dimmer depths of the room that was furnished with an oak roll-top desk, a swivel chair, and a long, leather-covered sofa. A huge brass spittoon sat beside the desk.

Wickware sat in the swivel chair with his booted feet on the desk. He didn't look like a lawyer. He looked more like a lawman, or a well-to-do cattleman. He was getting bald, paunchy, but there was sharp intelligence in his eyes.

He said: "Pull out a chair, Tom." Tom hooked a chair with his boot and pulled it toward him. Straddling it, he sat down, leaning his arms on its back. He said: "Geier didn't post a single handbill except in Adams City. They're all laying in a wash out on the dump. That's the reason there weren't any bidders but him."

"The hell! You sure?"

"Uhn-huh. Now what do I do about it?"

Wickware scratched his nose. He grunted regretfully: "Not a damned thing. Geier discharged his responsibility when he posted notices in Adams City. You can't touch him for not covering the country with them."

Tom snorted, angered. "Now's a hell of a fine time to tell me that."

"You didn't ask before," Wickware said gently, then went on: "Normally, nobody has to worry about it. The bank should have seen to it that it was done in their own interest as well as yours. The auctioneer should have seen to it that it was done, if only from the standpoint of his commission. Somebody slipped up, I guess."

"Yeah. Somebody slipped up, all right. Somebody slipped up and I'm out the difference between what Anchor's worth and Geier's lousy mortgage. Hell, Wickware, I don't know about these things. I've been raised as a cowman, not a lawyer. I've been going crazy ever since old Bob died. I couldn't seem to think of anything until the funeral was over. Then Geier came around and told me there was a past-due mortgage on Anchor. I tried to get a drive started, but he stopped me. You know all that."

As Wickware nodded, Tom heard steps ascending the outside staircase. He said bitterly: "There's nothing I can do then, legally?"

"Not a thing. Not a damned thing, Tom."

"Then I'll do it some other way."

A short, stout, tightly corseted woman came from the landing outside into the office. She was breathing hard. She gave Tom a reserved smile as he offered her his chair.

She said to Wickware: "I was down at Ringold's, and I thought I'd come up and wait until you were ready to go home." Her eyes flicked Otis. "How are you, Tom?" She sank into the chair.

He said—"I'm fine, Missus Wickware."—thinking that her tone was considerably less cordial than it had been the last time he'd seen her.

"What are you going to do, Tom?"

He shrugged. "Haven't had time to think about

it." He could feel anger stirring again, an anger all the more violent because it was so helpless.

Nora Wickware saw the resentment in his twisting face and said sharply: "Nothing foolish, I hope."

Tom said sourly, more so than he intended, and sarcastically: "No, of course not. Nothing foolish. Let him take Anchor away from me, but don't do anything foolish. What do you mean by foolish, Missus Wickware? Killing Geier?"

Wickware said reprovingly: "Tom."

"I'm sorry. But why is everybody so damned worried about Geier?" Tom Otis knew he was getting nowhere here, and admitted that it was probably his own fault. He went to the door. "Good bye," he said, and stepped out onto the landing.

As he went down the stairs, he was conscious of the uneasy silence behind him. His wild rage of the afternoon was gone, but his anger was not gone. Nor was the desire to do something, anything, to lessen the shock of realization that he was helpless.

At the bottom of the stairs he paused, fished his tobacco from his pocket, and rolled a cigarette. He touched a match to it.

The sun was fully down now, but the clouds above the mesa in the west were red-gold, flaming. A girl came out of Ringold's and started toward the stairway. She was a younger, slimmer edition of Mrs. Wickware and because of her youth was prettier, but in twenty years she would look as her mother looked now. She saw Tom, and for an instant the smile froze on her face. She recovered and turned to him.

"Tom!" Lucy Wickware exclaimed. "I had hoped I'd see you. Will you come to supper tonight?"

He could not have explained the reluctance he felt. He ought to appreciate this evidence that his losing Anchor made no difference in the way this girl felt toward him. Yet there was something wrong, and he couldn't put his finger on it.

Lucy said: "Well?"

Tom Otis smiled a little. That gentle impatient tone. Just like her mother's. He said: "You sort of took me by surprise. I guess I've had too much on my mind this afternoon."

Suddenly he had it, what had bothered him a few minutes before. It was Lucy's mother. At another time she would have asked Tom to supper herself, but she hadn't. Well, why should he blame her for that? Wasn't it natural for a mother to want security and plenty for her daughter? Maybe Mrs. Wickware was waiting to see what Tom would do, how he would take what had happened to him.

He said: "Some other time, Lucy. Thanks just the same."

She could hardly conceal her relief. Tom's lips

tightened. She stood for just a moment more, plainly uncomfortable.

At last she said: "Tom, we're all so sorry for what happened this afternoon. Have you any plans?"

He shook his head. He had no plans. All he had was anger, and resentment. Maybe that would be enough. Maybe plans would come later.

He said: "I haven't had time to make any plans. But I'm not going to tuck my tail between my legs and slink out of town, if that's what you mean."

Lucy put a hand on his arm. "Don't do anything foolish, Tom."

The repetition of her mother's caution suddenly angered him more. But he said nothing. Lucy gazed into his face a moment longer, then turned and ran up the stairs to her father's office.

Tom had been going with Lucy for more than a year. Almost everyone had taken it for granted they'd be married. He had accepted the idea himself, with some pleasure if not with outright enthusiasm. Now the complexity of his own feelings puzzled him. The Wickwares, mother and daughter, had made it plain enough in their indirect way that he was no longer particularly eligible. Perhaps he should have felt relieved, but he did not. Instead, he knew a combined feeling of hurt and increased resentment. It was hard to face the knowledge that his position and possessions were the main reasons for the liking and respect that his friends had for him.

He turned toward the river, feeling the need for a drink. Down at the end of town, he could see the big black and white sign of the Ute Saloon. Color faded from the clouds as he walked, and by the time he reached the saloon, purple dusk lay over the town. The heat of the day lessened, and became the pleasant warmth of a summer evening.

The saloon was almost deserted. One man stood at the bar, the big, black-bearded auctioneer. He turned to look at Tom, but instantly glanced back to the bottle before him.

Tom stepped up to the bar ten feet away from him.

The proprietor, Noah Shults, white-aproned and clean-shaven, moved along the bar, bringing a bottle and glass. He poured a drink and set it before Tom.

He said in a low tone: "That was a damned dirty steal this afternoon, Tom. What you going to do about it?"

Tom shrugged. "What can I do?" He was beginning to recognize the extreme danger of giving vent to his feelings. A man did not go around making threats if he had any sense. He drank the whiskey at a gulp and Noah poured him another, clucking sympathetically.

At a movement to his right, Tom glanced

toward the auctioneer. A sudden thought struck him. He picked up his glass and the bottle and moved along the bar.

The auctioneer's eyes widened with something that looked like fear.

Tom said: "Friend, I'd like to discuss the matter of your commission on that sale this afternoon. I found about a hundred handbills up at the dump on the edge of town. That means Geier didn't advertise the auction properly. It means that instead of your getting a commission on forty or fifty thousand dollars, you got a commission on ten. What do you think of that?"

The man wet his thick lips. He stood a full inch taller than Tom, weighed a full fifty pounds more. But a lot of that was fat.

He mumbled: "I'm not complaining. I guess such things happen." Hastily he tossed off his drink and turned toward the door, saying lamely: "Well, I've got a long ride to make."

But Tom caught his arm. His grip was savage.

He said: "Damn you, don't walk away when I'm talking to you!"

The auctioneer began to bluster. He yanked away, and, as Tom moved to close with him again, the auctioneer's fist made solid contact with his jaw. The man's whole two hundred pounds was behind the blow, and Tom staggered back.

The pain of the blow went unnoticed, though,

in the sudden surge of triumph that he felt. He began to grin, and stepped in close. Here was something a man could fight. And once the fight was over, there was something here to be learned.

III

Noah Shults yelled—"Hey!"—but it was a futile protest. Tom's left smacked cleanly against the auctioneer's bearded jaw. His eyes were narrowed, and action seemed to release all the pent-up tension in his tight-strung nerves in one glorious instant. He bored in, taking the flurry of the big man's blows impartially on his shoulders and head. His right cocked up and smashed solidly against the big man's cheek bone.

The auctioneer staggered back against a table. Tom followed, but the big man felt the back of a chair with his hands behind him, and was raising it as he brought it around. Tom tried to stop, but, when he saw he could not, he raised his arms, and took part of the blow's force on them. His right arm went numb as a chair rung crashed against it.

The chair drove his arms down, and shattered on his head. Tom went to his knees. Immediately the big man came on, his knee raising to smash Tom's jaw. Tom dived aside, rolled back, and with both arms took the auctioneer's feet out from under him.

He got up, still staggered by that blow from the chair. The big man lumbered to his feet. As he straightened, Tom moved in and delivered a slashing flurry of blows to eyes and jaw. Blood welled from a gash over the auctioneer's left eye. Blood streamed from his nose.

Tom ducked one of his wild swings, and came in again. His fists drove like steam pistons, with lightning regularity. There was no pausing and no hesitation in Tom Otis now. The smack of his fists was like the rolling of a drum. The auctioneer tried to put up a defense, but Tom kept him off balance, driving him back, forcing him to cover up, with no retaliation.

With the man's back against the bar, Tom paused for the briefest instant, cocking his right back and bringing it forward and up with all the strength of his shoulder and back behind it. It landed on the side of the bearded giant's jaw with a crack that could have been heard in the street. The auctioneer's eyes crossed, and glazed, and he slumped down against the bar.

Tom was panting hard. He leaned on the bar for a moment, drawing great, gasping breaths of air into his lungs.

The auctioneer stirred, and groaned. Tom yanked him to his feet. Beneath his sweaty shirt his muscles corded and bulged with the effort.

He propped the auctioneer against the bar and spoke, his words clipped and short.

He said: "You act like you were in on the whole thing."

The man shook his head dumbly.

Tom shrugged. "All right. We'll try it again. Only there won't be any knockout blows. I'll just beat the rest of you to a pulp."

The auctioneer's eyes were watching him with a kind of dazed, animal cunning. His hand snaked under his coat for his gun. Tom caught the hand as it came out, swung around, bringing the hand up over his shoulder. He stooped, bringing the hand down violently. He felt a crack as he dislocated the elbow, then the auctioneer flew over his head and across the room. The gun, a two-shot Derringer, clattered to the floor at his feet.

Walking easily, Tom crossed the room. The auctioneer stared up at him like a whipped dog. His eyes were red, slitted, and venomous.

Tom said: "Ready to talk about it now?"

For a moment defiance lingered in the auctioneer, but when it went, it went with a rush.

Tom asked: "Geier took care of you on the commission deal, is that it?"

The man nodded.

Tom asked: "How much did you get?"

"A thousand dollars."

"What do you usually work for on a deal this size?"

"Two percent."

Tom looked toward the bar. He said: "You heard him, Noah. He got a thousand dollars for a ten-thousand-dollar sale. But a thousand dollars is two percent of fifty thousand. That's what Anchor should have brought. That . . . and more."

Suddenly Tom had a feeling that someone was watching him. His back was to the door, and he swung around uneasily. Don Yarbo, the sheriff, stood just inside the batwings.

Tom said: "You heard it, too, didn't you, Sheriff?"

The sheriff nodded. Tom swung back to the auctioneer. He said: "Get out of here! Ride while I feel like letting you."

The auctioneer slinked out of the saloon. The doors closed behind him. Tom thought: *I'm getting somewhere now.*

Yarbo's eyes were cold. He was a small man, cocky as a banty rooster. He wore a single gun low on his right side, tied to his thigh. His gold-plated star shone brightly in the lamp glow as he stroked his long brown mustache.

He said: "You pull anything more like this and I'll throw you in jail. You're a sorehead about Anchor, but you better slow down unless you want to stretch rope."

Yarbo's words were like coal oil dumped upon the smoldering coals of Tom's anger. It flamed into raging fury. Blood crimsoned Tom's face. There was no restraint and no caution left in him. Only blind, savage rage. All he could think was: *Geier's even got the law in his pocket.*

He came across the saloon floor in a foolish, furious rush. Yarbo stepped back. His hand snaked down after the gun, fast as light. The gun was out and raised when Tom Otis came within range. It glinted dull blue as it flashed downward.

The barrel cracked hard against Tom's skull. Before his eyes light flashed briefly, crazily, and then the darkness came. . . .

When Tom came to, he recognized the sharp, unpleasant odor of disinfectant. And he knew immediately that he was in jail, for that was the only place around where that odor could be found. Tom had never been there before himself, but he'd bailed out Anchor cowpunchers often enough after a pay-day drunk.

He was lying on a bare cot. The wire springs of the cot bit cruelly into his flesh. He sat up, swinging his feet to the floor. A thousand sledges began beating against his skull and his vision blurred. He dropped his head into his hands.

Across the cell, on the other cot, another man was snoring softly. Tom raised his head and looked at him, but didn't recognize the man.

He'd never seen him before. He was a big man, red-haired, unshaven, and dirty.

Tom thought—*Saddle tramp.*—and dismissed the fellow from his thoughts.

He got up and wandered to the window. From the position of the sun, he judged that it must be near 10:00 a.m. He'd been out cold for over fourteen hours. That was some whack Yarbo had given him.

Gradually the events of the past day began to come back. The auction, Lily, the auctioneer. Last night he'd thought he was getting some-where. Now he doubted it. How could he get anywhere when the man who had robbed him had all of the law on his side?

A chair squeaked in the jail office, and Tom heard the door open. He heard a low murmur of voices—Yarbo's, a woman's, another man's. He couldn't distinguish words.

But after a few moments of that, Yarbo came to the cell door and unlocked it. He asked sourly: "Drunk all slept off?"

Tom scowled at him. He said: "Damn you, you know I wasn't drunk."

Yarbo only shrugged. He grunted—"Come on."—and stood aside while Tom staggered from the cell.

Tom went through the open door and into the sheriff's office. Lily Street stood there, watching him, and just behind her was old Doc Willis.

Lily said: "Sit down, Tom. Doc wants to look at your head." There was compassion in her eyes, but there was anger, too, lurking in their depths.

Tom began to understand. Lily had missed him this morning, and had made some inquiries. Noah had probably told her about what had happened. Lily had come to the jail to see him and he'd still been unconscious. So Lily had gone after the doctor.

It was as simple as that, but Tom looked at Lily with something different in his eyes.

Doc Willis said gruffly: "Sit down. You're damn' near six inches taller than I am. How can I see your head 'way up there?"

Tom sat down. Yarbo slumped down into his swivel chair, scowling fiercely.

Doc Willis probed at the bump on Tom's head with gentle fingers, but even so it hurt like hell. It made the flashing lights reel around in front of his eyes again. Doc opened one of Tom's eyes with thumb and forefingers and stared into it.

He straightened. "Concussion. Bad one." He turned to the sheriff, his voice accusing. "Tom could have died in there last night. You're damned lucky he didn't." He looked back at Tom. "Think you can walk over to the hotel?"

Yarbo sprang to his feet. "Wait a minute! I didn't say he could go. He jumped me last night. I'm going to hold him a while."

Doc snorted. Tom stood up. He looked from

34

the sheriff to Doc and back again. Doc said: "Release him to my . . ."

Lily interrupted: "Wait a minute, Doc." She walked over to the sheriff's desk. Her voice was soft, silky, as she said: "I'm not asking you to release him, Sheriff. I'm telling you to. Don't you understand that?"

Yarbo flushed and began to tug at his mustache. "Well, hell, if it's that important. Well, sure, Lily."

Tom was becoming increasingly puzzled as Lily said to Yarbo: "Get him his gun and whatever else you took away from him last night."

The sheriff shuffled across the office. He got Tom's gun and belt down off a board and took a pocket knife and some keys and small change out of a drawer. He handed these to Tom with a surly scowl on his face.

Tom shoved the knife and coins into his pocket. He belted on the gun and followed Lily out into the blinding heat, into the dazzling sunlight. Again pain shot through his head. He blinked his eyes, held them slitted to let in a minimum of light.

Getting to the hotel was a kind of nightmare. His thoughts fuzzed and blurred. But once there and in a room he remembered Doc clipping hair from his skull, washing and bandaging the gaping wound there. He recalled Lily leaving the room while he slipped out of his clothes.

Then he was on the bed, and sinking into the intoxicating, cushioned void of sleep.

He dreamed of Lily Street, the dance-hall singer, warm and tight against him. He dreamed of Lily Street with the hardness of steel in her voice. He dreamed of Lily Street, whose unsuspected influence could make the sheriff, against his will, release a prisoner.

In his dreams, she was all human qualities assembled in one person—compassion, love, gentleness, guile, power, and ruthlessness. And when he awoke at dark, it was with Lily Street in his mind.

He lay and thought about her. Her concern for him was not based on either love or simple compassion. He was convinced of that. Lily wanted something, something that only Tom Otis could give her.

And what was that? He shook his head, surprised that it no longer ached. He hadn't an answer to his question, but he had a feeling that it would not be long in coming.

IV

Tom Otis lay on the bed, reluctant to move for a long time. It seemed good to be still and quiet. He heard the night sounds begin out in the Adams City streets. He heard a bunch of

Anchor cowpunchers come whooping into town, recognizing their voices. He heard the bell on the courthouse toll 7:00. It occurred to him suddenly that this was Saturday night.

He got up cautiously, but, except for an odd, light feeling in his head, everything seemed normal. He pulled the shade and touched a match to the lamp wick. The chimney was sooty, but he didn't try to clean it.

He went over and stared at himself in the cracked mirror. Thick yellow stubble covered his face. His eyes were bloodshot. He grinned when he saw the way his head was swathed with bandages.

Slipping into his trousers and boots, he poured cold water from a pitcher into a basin and washed. He was drying his face when he heard a knock on the door. But before he answered it, he belted on his gun. Then he flung the door open quickly, ready.

Lily stood there, smiling. "Still alive?" She stepped inside, closed the door behind her. "I was getting worried about you."

"I think I'll live."

Lily's beauty, in spite of the worldly-wisdom in her eyes, was lively and striking, vivid. Her lips were full and red, her teeth gleamed white, her eyes were bright. She was dressed for work in a low-cut satin gown. Her shoulders and the exposed part of her breasts were creamy

37

and smooth. Her breath came just a little fast, probably from the climb upstairs.

When a woman wants to be kissed, it is unmistakable. Tom Otis reached for her, and she came to him willingly, eagerly. Instead of stirring Tom, though, the kiss angered him. He bore down harder, bruising her lips, crushing her against him with all his strength.

When he released her, he looked down at her and said harshly: "You've been in Adams City for more than a year. In all that time I never got closer to you than five feet. Isn't this kind of sudden? And kind of unusual? 'Most everybody else I know seems to have sort of lost interest in me since I lost Anchor. Odd, but you didn't want much to do with me when I had the ranch. Now, all of a sudden, you're about the only friend I have, and you're interested in hearts and flowers, too. What's the deal?"

He had acted brutally and he had spoken brutally. But Lily only smiled. She stepped over to the mirror and patted her hair into place. When she turned back, her eyes showed him her approval.

She said: "Geier's the deal." Suddenly her eyes lost their softness and became hard and hating.

Comprehension began to come to Tom. Lily hated Geier, too. Lily had her own axe to grind, and she wanted Tom Otis to turn the grindstone. Refusal was on the tip of his tongue, then he recalled the calm way Lily had ordered Yarbo to release him this morning. Had it not been for her, he'd still be lying in that stinking cell.

Also, he had got a pretty good glimpse of the way the cards were stacked against him. He had glimpsed failure for himself plainly enough in the way Geier had the steal of Anchor rigged. An ally could do him no harm, and might make possible what he could not accomplish alone.

He began to grin. "You hate him, too, then? Mind telling me why?"

Lily shook her head. Her eyes were as hard as agate. "You don't need to know that. It's enough that, for the moment, our interests seem to be the same. I help you, and you help me. Is it a deal?"

He shrugged. "All right." He crossed the room and got his shirt, slipped it on, and tucked it into his pants. He went back to Lily and stood looking down at her. "Maybe I won't be as much help as you expect. Right now, I'm wandering around in a box cañon. Damned if I can see the way out."

Lily smiled enigmatically. "There's a way." She turned and opened the door. "I've got to go to work. I'll meet you down by the river where we were yesterday a little after midnight. Then we can talk about it."

"All right." He watched her go, hips swaying slightly, shoulders straight. He scratched his bearded face.

He got his hat and tried it on. He couldn't pull it down over the bandages. Shrugging, he sailed it onto the bed and went out, closing the door.

In the hotel lobby he passed half a dozen men who were supposed to be his friends. Four of them studiously avoided seeing him. The other two nodded shortly.

Outside, he paused long enough to roll a cigarette and light it. In the match flare, his face was somber, bitter. He dropped the match and crossed the street to the barbershop.

There was a man in the chair, his face hidden by a steaming towel, and two men were waiting on the long bench. One was Hal Boyd, foreman of Anchor. He threw down the paper he was reading, and a broad grin suddenly spread over his face.

"Tom! Boy, how you making it?"

He moved aside to make room and Tom sat down beside him. Tom shrugged, smiling. Boyd's steadfastness gave him a warm feeling he had not felt since he'd lost Anchor. It restored a good bit of his faith in human nature, lost so completely these past two days. It told him that all friendship was not based on what a man owns.

"What you going to do, Tom?" asked Boyd.

"Get a job, I reckon. I haven't thought about it too much. I've been trying to figure a way out of the fix I'm in." He told Boyd quickly about the steal that Geier had rigged, and ended: "I'm flat broke, except for what's in my pockets. Dad let what we had in the bank dwindle down to nothing. He was operating on credit altogether just before he was killed."

"Did Geier take on Anchor's debts?" Boyd inquired.

Tom laughed bitterly. "What do you think?" He shook his head. "No. That'll be up to me, I reckon. But I'm damned if I know how I'll ever get them paid on a 'puncher's wages."

Thinking of Anchor's debts, of his own wealth—the few coins in his pocket—suddenly made Tom think of something else. He said: "Wait a minute! Wait a minute. I just thought of something."

"What?" Hal Boyd was puzzled.

"My TO brand. Hal, I've just remembered my TO cattle. They're mine, and they don't go with Anchor."

When Tom had been fourteen, his father had begun paying him wages, and he had begun doing a man's work on Anchor. During the summer months, when he hadn't been in school, he'd drawn wages. Only old Bob had given him his wages in cattle. A yearling heifer for every month he worked. And Tom had branded them TO, the initials of his name.

As the years had passed, his small herd had increased. He'd traded his bull calves to his

41

father for heifer calves. They were his own, those TO cattle, yet he had never really considered them his own. He'd thought of them as part of Anchor, just as he himself was part of Anchor. They had eaten Anchor grass and had run with Anchor herds.

Tom said thoughtfully: "Geier's never going to agree that they're mine."

Hal Boyd agreed, grinning. "No, sir. Not Geier."

"Then I'll take them. If I try to go through the courts to get them, it'll take ten years, and by that time Geier'd see to it that there weren't any left."

Boyd laid a hand on his arm. "Don't talk so damned loud. You know how fast news travels in this town."

Tom said—"You're right."—but he wasn't thinking about that. He was feeling a sudden, soaring, searing excitement. He'd been in a box cañon and hadn't seen any way out. But this changed things. A man who wasn't broke, wasn't beat!

The man in the barber chair got up and went over to the mirror and began to put on his tie. Harvey Reuter, clerk in Ringold's store. He nodded at Tom as he went out. Hal Boyd took the chair.

Tom sat, staring at the floor. The more he thought about it, the less question remained in his mind. He had thought of the cattle more as Anchor cattle than his own. But they weren't Anchor cattle. They were Tom Otis's cattle, taken as wages for his work through the years. He tried to remember what the TO count had been last year. Something over four hundred, he remembered.

Damn it, damn it, damn it! Why hadn't he thought of the TO cattle before? Then he remembered that Geier had refused to allow him time for a drive. He couldn't have got the TO cattle any quicker than he could Anchor cattle. Even if he'd thought about them, he would still have been unable to save Anchor.

But the TO cattle gave him something to fight with. He was frowning with concentration when Hal Boyd got out of the chair. The other man who had been waiting had left, apparently tired of waiting.

Tom told Hal—"Wait for me."—and, as he got into the chair, he was thinking that if he could round up a crew on promises, he could start tomorrow to gather his TO cattle. They were scattered from one end of Anchor to the other, and it would take either a damned good crew or a lot of time to get them. He'd never get them all, but he'd probably get most of them.

The barber dropped the chair back and began to lather his face. He put steaming towels on it, took them off, and lathered up again. Boyd had gone back to reading his newspaper. The barber shaved Tom quickly, expertly. He put stinging bay rum on Tom's face, and Tom got out of the chair.

When Tom went out of the shop with Hal Boyd, the street was busy. It was not yet 8:00, and Ringold's was still open. Tom sat down on the bench in front of the barbershop. Boyd sat down beside him and began to roll a smoke.

Tom said: "How many of the crew will quit Anchor and pitch in with me?"

Boyd was thoughtful. He was apparently shuffling the members of the crew in his mind. Finally he said: "I think I can count on four of them."

Tom smiled. Four wasn't many out of twenty. But it was a hell of a lot more than none. And it was enough. He said: "I won't be able to pay any of you until the job's done. So it's kind of speculative."

Hal Boyd shrugged, grinning. "When do we start?"

"Tomorrow morning."

Boyd got up. He was almost a head shorter than Tom, was broad and squat. Nearing forty, he was beginning to put pounds over the lean, tough rawhide of his muscles. But the muscles were still there. His face was broad and cheerful. Except for a little hair at each side of his head, he was bald.

He took off his hat, scrubbed his baldpate with his knuckles, and said: "I'll be riding, then. Where you want to meet us?"

"At the head of the Ute Trail. We'll start there and work back toward Blue River. We'll take 'em out on that side. We can drive to the railroad at Arnoldsville."

"We'll be there."

Boyd strode off in the direction of the livery stable. Tom sat, watching the crowd stream past in the street. He looked across at the darkened windows of the bank. He didn't know exactly what he hoped to accomplish by this roundup and drive, but he knew that at least he'd be doing something. He'd be getting something that belonged to him, perhaps even the means of striking back at Geier.

He got up and strolled across the street toward the Colorado Saloon where Lily Street worked, unaware that a man was watching him from a dark passageway between the Colorado Saloon and the saddle shop next door.

V

At least twice as big as the Ute, the Colorado was the fanciest saloon in Adams City. It was the only saloon in town that boasted both gambling tables and dancing girls. On Saturday night, it filled up about 9:00 and kept running that way right up until 1:00 a.m., closing time. But Lily got off at midnight.

As Tom stepped into the light that shone into the street from the windows of the Colorado, an odd feeling of uneasiness assailed him. He glanced quickly to right and left, seeing nothing. But as his eyes flicked back to the door of the Colorado, he caught the gleam of light on metal from the corner of his eye.

Instantly his full glance went to that spot. The glint was gone, but a shadow figure that lurked there between the two buildings was not.

It took but an instant for his mind to realize that a man who would lurk in darkness like that was potentially dangerous. And with that realization came the memory of that glint of light on metal.

Feeling foolish, but somehow compelled, Tom jumped quickly to one side, drawing his own gun. A flash blossomed in the dark passageway, and sharp pain seared along Tom's side. His gun centered on the passageway, and he triggered two fast shots at the flash. Then he jumped aside again, quickly.

He heard the sound of running feet from the mouth of the passageway. Though reluctant, he ran into the passageway. Behind him he heard a shout. A quick, over-the-shoulder glance showed him a group collecting in the mouth of the passageway. Ahead of him, the footsteps were receding. He stopped and went back to the street.

Lily was there, and Mike McGill, owner of the Colorado. There were a dozen or more other people, too—ranchers, cowpunchers, storekeepers.

Tom said: "Somebody took a shot at me."

He'd been calm enough during the shooting, but now his hands began to shake. He holstered his gun, felt of his side, and grimaced with pain. Lily pulled him into the Colorado. She took him back through the saloon to Mike McGill's office, sat down, and pulled out his shirt tail as though she owned him. She got a towel and mopped at his bloody side.

Tom yelped: "Ouch! Damn it, be careful!"

Her voice was sharp. "An inch to the left and I wouldn't have to be careful."

She dampened the towel and sponged off the blood, poured whiskey on the wound, and put a clean towel on for a compress. Then she tucked back his shirt tail to hold the towel in place.

She was smiling now. "Painful but hardly serious. Who did it?"

"How do I know? He got away."

"What've you been up to since I saw you last? Why should Geier want to kill you?"

"Who said it was Geier?"

"I said it was." And she repeated: "What's happened since I last saw you?"

Tom stared at her. He glared, growing angry,

and not quite knowing why. Maybe it was the way she talked to him. Maybe it was her cool assurance. Maybe it was only his own confusion.

He said: "I went to the barbershop for a shave. I ran into Hal Boyd there, and we got to talking."

"What about?"

"TO cattle."

"What brand is that?"

He told her: "My own brand. Geier can't claim my TO cattle belong with Anchor. Hal and I decided to make a gather and drive all the TO stuff we could find to the railroad at Arnoldsville." Lily was frowning, so Tom said somewhat defensively: "They're mine. There's around five hundred of them. They'd bring me close to ten thousand in Denver."

"And you decided all this in the barbershop?" Her tone had become contemptuous. "Who was there besides you two?"

Tom's anger increased, but he forced himself to speak quietly. "Harvey Reuter. The barber. Another *hombre* . . ." He frowned.

Lily asked: "What's the matter?"

"That one got tired of waiting and left."

"Who was he?"

Tom frowned. "I don't know his name. He lives downriver about fifteen miles. Got a two-bit outfit and runs his cattle along the river bottom."

Mike McGill came in. He was a scrawny little

Irishman with a head of bushy white hair. His eyes were blue and guileless. When he wanted them to be. Right now they were sharp and shrewd.

"You know who shot you?" he demanded.

Tom shook his head. He stood up. "I'm all right now." He went to the door and Lily walked with him. In the hallway outside, she whispered—"Midnight."—and Tom nodded.

He went on out and found a seat at a table next to the wall. Lily Street came on for her first number about ten minutes later. She sang "Susanna," and afterward "Gentle Annie." Her voice was sweet and throaty. She was animated during the "Susanna" number, dreamy and sad as she sang "Gentle Annie." As always, the applause was thunderous.

Tom puzzled about her for a few moments, then his thoughts returned to Anchor and to Will Geier. There was only one believable explanation for the shooting tonight. The man in the barbershop had run to Geier with the news that Tom intended to gather TO cattle. And Geier had sent someone to kill him.

This was the first indication that Geier's position was not unassailable. Either Geier felt shaky, or he simply hated to lose the TO cattle to Tom. It was one or the other, or a combination of both. Geier would know that Tom Otis, broke, could hardly be any particular threat to his security. But Tom Otis with $10,000 in his jeans could be a considerable threat.

Either way, it added up that Geier would not stop with this single, abortive threat against his life. There would be other attempts. It was up to Tom, then, to walk carefully and see that none of them succeeded.

The saloon door banged open. Tom glanced toward the sound. He saw Will Geier standing there before the doors, searching the room with his black-browed, restless glance.

Geier did not look like a banker. He was younger than most bankers, for one thing. He was big, for another. His shoulders bulged against his black broadcloth coat. He wore a small mustache and his smile could be affable and winning. Just now it was not. It was cold and angry.

He saw Tom and wheeled toward him. Tom leaned back in his chair. Without waiting for an invitation, Geier came up to him, pulled out a chair, and sat down.

He said: "So you're sore about Anchor. Yarbo says you're making some wild accusations."

Tom grinned. He could not remember ever having seen Will Geier before when he was not confident and sure. Geier was neither just now.

Tom said—"Wild accusations?"—accenting the *wild*.

"Yes, wild. I hired a man to take these handbills

downriver, and I hired another to take them east. I paid each of them twenty-five dollars and their expenses to do it. Tom, it's not my fault they didn't do what they were paid to do."

Tom grinned tightly. "No, it isn't, is it? But it saved you close to forty thousand dollars. A good break for you, wasn't it?"

Geier flushed. He leaned forward, his eyes narrowed. He said: "Don't push me too far, Tom."

Otis grinned again. There was a tight feeling in his stomach, a tingling feeling in the back of his neck that he found oddly pleasant.

He said softly: "Geier, I'll push you right off Anchor."

Geier took a moment to digest this. Then he stood up, glaring down at the rancher. He started to turn away, but his anger was too much for him. He swung back and said in a low voice: "Don't try to take those TO cattle, Tom Otis." But his eyes showed his instant knowledge that he had gone too far.

Tom said, rising: "So that fellow in the barbershop did run to you. And you sent someone to kill me."

He moved out around the table, wanting more than anything else to smash his big fist into Geier's mouth. Geier backed away a couple of steps.

Tom didn't quite know what stopped him.

Some native caution, perhaps. Some remembrance of Yarbo and of Yarbo's stinking jail. If he started a row with Geier now, it would be just what the man wanted. So he held himself still, saying only: "You're afraid of me, aren't you, Geier? So afraid, you'd hire a man to kill me."

"You're crazy! You haven't got anything I want. Why should I want you dead?" Geier scowled, whirled around, marched to the doors, and banged through them. Tom watched the doors swing for a moment, then he followed.

He walked slowly through the Saturday night crowd toward the livery barn. He supposed someone had put his horse up after he'd been thrown in jail. Noah Shults probably.

There was a kid on duty at the stable. A kid of about thirteen. His voice was a kid's voice, but changing, and every once in a while it broke and gave off a couple of deep notes. Whenever it did, the kid would flush painfully.

He said: "Sure, Mister Otis. Your horse is here. Noah Shults brought him night before last. I'll get him for you."

He went back into the gloomy stable and after several minutes returned, leading Tom's horse. Tom mounted and rode out into the street.

He didn't have anything particular to do between now and midnight, and he didn't feel like drinking. He didn't much feel like company, either, so he decided to ride down along the river a way.

He was heading down a side street toward the edge of town when a call came out of the darkness to him.

"Tom!"

A woman's voice. Lucy Wickware's voice. He was passing the Wickware house. Lucy must have been sitting on the porch. He reined over.

Lucy came down the walk to the gate. Out of courtesy and not because he wanted to, Tom dismounted. He pulled his reins through the brass ring on the hitching post.

Lucy waited until he reached the gate before she spoke. "Tom. Dad says you've been seeing Lily Street."

"Seeing her?" He laughed. "She got me out of jail, if that's what you mean."

"Are you in love with her?"

Suddenly this struck Tom Otis as ridiculously funny. Lucy had been relieved the other night when he'd refused her supper invitation. Her mother had made it rather plain that without Anchor he was not a particularly desirable catch for Lucy, so far as she was concerned. Yet an overtone in Lucy's voice now was plainly caused by jealousy.

Tom said: "No, I'm not in love with her, nor she with me. Although I can't see why that should interest you."

53

Lucy was silent for a moment. Then she asked: "Aren't you being unnecessarily cruel?" Tom shrugged, and Lucy said: "I hear you're going to get your own TO cattle."

"Where'd you hear that?"

"Dad was talking about it. He said he heard it in Ringold's store."

Tom felt a surge of resentful anger. He said: "Lucy, don't straddle the fence. Get on one side of it or the other and stay there." He turned away, and untied his horse.

Lucy pleaded—"Tom, wait!"—but Tom swung up to his saddle without answering. He rode off into the darkness without looking back.

Her about-face was occasioned then by the belief that he was still reasonably well-fixed. A man with $10,000 in cash was not a total loss so far as the Wickware women were concerned. His sudden understanding of Lucy and her mother left a bitter, sour taste in his mouth.

He cursed softly and kicked his horse into a crazy run.

VI

On the stroke of midnight, Tom Otis was at the appointed spot for his rendezvous with Lily Street. She came riding through the sage about fifteen minutes later. He got to his feet to help

54

her down, and she let him. His side was still sore, and the soreness was spreading, but he forgot pain in the excitement of Lily's nearness.

As she stood close to him, her elusive fragrance made his blood leap. Bitter and sour as his thoughts had been for the past couple of hours, he forgot them all when his arms closed about her.

It was obviously what she had wanted, for she came closer with a little cry. He lowered his lips to hers, and it was like a match touched to dry powder. Her body was soft, pliant, but strong with her desire. He picked her up in his arms, carried her toward a grassy spot on the bank.

Her voice was small, frightened: "What are you going to do?"

"Just what you think I'm going to do." He laid her down on the grassy bank, lowered himself beside her. He found her stiff, resisting.

She said: "Tom, don't rush me. Please!"

His voice was harsh. He was tired of being pushed back and forth by the women in his life, pushed like a pawn on a chessboard. Lucy Wickware had rejected him, then tried to get him back in the course of forty-eight hours. Lily had played up to him deliberately for some selfish purpose of her own because she hated Geier.

He said: "I suppose you're going to tell me you've never . . ."

She interrupted: "That would be funny,

wouldn't it? That would be a scream! A dance-hall girl who has never slept with a man?"

Tom growled, oddly disturbed: "It'd be damned unusual. Are you trying to tell me it's so?"

Lily pulled away from him and sat up. "No, I'm not telling you that. You wouldn't believe it anyway, would you?"

He started to shake his head. But he wasn't sure. Puzzlement made him frown. "I don't know. Maybe I would."

He told himself that he was a fool. But there had been a ring of truth in Lily's voice. He fished out his tobacco and shook flakes of it into a tiny trough of paper, rolled it carefully.

He said: "What the hell do you want from me, Lily? Tell me what you want. Maybe you don't have to buy my help."

Lily was silent for so long that he thought she wasn't going to answer. He touched a match to the cigarette end and in its flare looked at Lily. She was crying silently.

He said: "Is my gathering the TO cattle going to upset your plans?"

"Oh, Tom, I was going to use you. I was going to egg you into helping me. But I can't do it. I can't!"

"What did you want me to do?"

"I was going to get you to rob Geier's bank. I was going to get you all worked up, then suggest it. After that I was going ahead with my plan."

56

"What plan?"

Her voice was almost inaudible. "Do you mind if I don't tell you, Tom? Can you trust me now? Nothing I'm planning will hurt you. Honest, Tom. Go ahead and sell your cattle. Bring the money back. If I'm lucky with my plan, you'll get your ranch back."

"Mind telling me how?" He was frankly skeptical, faintly suspicious.

"I can't tell you, Tom. It isn't that I don't trust you. But if even a hint of what I'm planning gets out, it won't work. You go ahead and sell your cattle. You'll have most of what Geier's mortgage amounted to. I think it will be enough."

"What are you going to get out of it?"

Lily shrugged. In the faint starlight and the glow from his cigarette, he could see the light, sad, enigmatic smile on her full lips. She said: "Nothing now. I had hoped to get revenge against Geier."

"Revenge for what?"

He could sense the stiffening of her body. "It's a long story. I won't bore you with it. Geier swindled my father out of a ranch almost as big as yours, a ranch that my grandfather started from nothing soon after the Civil War. It broke my father, and he killed himself."

She sat, staring moodily out across the whispering river. For a moment, Tom sat utterly still.

Then he said: "You're a strange girl. You know you've got me puzzled, don't you?"

"You won't be puzzled long."

Tom thought of Sheriff Don Yarbo. He said: "You made the sheriff turn me loose. How'd you do that?"

Lily's answer was listless. "Blackmail. I know of a killing that Yarbo is wanted for. He hasn't always been a lawman. He used to be a cheap tinhorn gunman. It's probably not the only place he's wanted."

Tom was puzzled as to what Lily's plan could be, and how she intended to go about recovering the ranch. To him it seemed impossible, yet she seemed to be sure. He said: "So you've been kicking around trying to make a living since your father's death. You've had it pretty rugged, haven't you?"

Lily shrugged, smiling. She stood up. "No, it hasn't been too bad. You get used to things."

She walked back to where her horse was standing. Tom helped her up to her saddle, then found his own horse and mounted. He rode beside her toward the scattered, dim lights of the town.

When they reached the hotel, they dismounted together. The street was nearly deserted now. The Colorado would be closing in a few minutes. Tom was again wondering what steps Geier would take to see that he failed to gather and

58

ship his TO cattle, when he said mechanically: "I'll take your horse around to the stable."

Lily stepped close to him. Subdued and quiet, she looked up at him for a long time. It was as though she were searching for something in his face. At last she said: "Will you kiss me good bye, Tom?"

He gathered her in his arms. When he stepped away, his pulses again were pounding, his face was flushed. He said: "Lily, when I get back . . ."

Lily said: "All right, Tom. When you get back." She ran lightly into the hotel.

Tom stared after her for a moment, wanting her. Then he caught the reins of her horse and, holding them, mounted his own animal. He rode along the side of the hotel, through the weed-grown vacant lot toward the stable at the rear of the hotel.

His mind was concerned only with Lily. But as he rode this short distance, he cooled, and abruptly became uneasily alert. Geier had planted one killer tonight. And while Tom did not believe he would try the same method again so soon, he nevertheless did not relax his vigilance.

Reaching the stable, he handed the reins of Lily's horse down to the hostler. He returned the way he had come to the street, and headed at a slow lope out of town toward Anchor.

He had a long ride, an all-night ride ahead of

him if he was to be at the head of the Ute Trail at daybreak. But his spirits began to lift as he rode. This was action, movement, doing something.

This was a relief after the waiting, the helpless brooding. And when this job was done, he could come back to Adams City and begin the final battle toward regaining Anchor.

What he did not know was that Will Geier, driving a buggy, had left Adams City for Anchor nearly two hours before. What he did not know was that Geier, suspicious and frightened, would now go to any lengths to see that Tom Otis failed to load a single TO steer on the train at Arnoldsville.

As the hours of the night wore on, and Tom Otis drew nearer and nearer the Ute Trail, even through the darkness he could note the difference in the terrain.

The land atop the high mesa was like a different country compared to that around Adams City. Here, aspen groves laid a dappled shade on the lush grass. Springs bubbled up in the draws and ran until they spilled off the rims. In the valley below, they fed the waters of Clear Creek that ran to its confluence with the river at Adams City.

Deer bounded away at Tom Otis's approach as he climbed up through the rim in the first gray light of dawn. He found Hal Boyd and his crew of four loyal Anchor cowpunchers squatted around a fire, brewing coffee. A couple of pack horses grazed nearby under full pack.

Tom rode close to the fire and dismounted. Hal rose, grinning, and handed him a tin cup of coffee that steamed in the early morning chill.

Tom looked around at his crew. There was Johnny MacIntosh, Anchor's oldest rider, stiff and sore with rheumatism and the early morning cold. There was Pete Fisk, a tall, good-natured Texan. There were two others who had been with Anchor as long as Tom Otis could remember— Eric Northcutt and Jack Lea.

There were no heroics or exhibitions of any kind. The men greeted Tom as they had greeted him every morning for over ten years, and they asked no questions. They did not even comment on the job they were to start today. It was as though Anchor had never changed hands, as though this were simply another task to be worked at steadily and without pause until it was accomplished.

Tom finished his coffee and dumped the dregs on the fire.

Hal Boyd yelled—"All right . . . let's get moving!"—and scattered the embers of the fire with his boot. With no confusion, the crew mounted.

Johnny MacIntosh was sent on ahead with the pack animals. At first, he grumbled, considering this a menial chore, until Hal told him: "The quickest way for Geier to stop us is to steal our grub. That's why I'm sending you with the pack horses, Johnny."

The mesa was shaped like a hand with the fingers spread. Each finger was a ridge, varying in length from five to ten miles. All Anchor range was fenced naturally by the rims, except for the back end, which was fenced with aspen poles. In some places, the rims were only forty or fifty feet high, but in others the sheer rock barriers dropped away for five or six hundred feet.

From the trail, the five rode southward to the point of the ridge, beginning their gather there. They would work perhaps halfway back on this ridge today, driving TO stock ahead of them as they went. Tomorrow, they would finish this ridge and start the next.

The ridges were easy. The main body of the mesa would not be so easy. Tom hoped that, if Geier intended to hit them, it would be while they were working the ridges, and not after they got strung out and separated on the main plateau.

VII

Pete Fisk and Tom worked the eastern side of the ridge, Hal and Eric Northcutt the west. Jack Lea rode down the center, taking each man's gather as it was brought in, six or eight head at a time, holding them in a slow-moving bunch.

Tom liked this work. He liked the feel of his horse under him, working with him. He liked the charging rush of the cattle as they broke out of the brush and tore off ahead of him. He liked the neat way his horse could cut a single TO animal out of a bunch and push it ahead.

He forgot Will Geier for a time, almost forgot Lily Street. He forgot that Anchor was no longer his. He forgot the danger that Geier presented.

They nooned a mile and a half beyond their morning camp. Tom looked at the morning's gather with satisfaction. Nearly thirty head. A much better gather from this ridge than he had expected.

He found firewood while Pete shaved a stick and started the fire. A hail brought Johnny out of the timber with the pack animals. Inside of fifteen minutes, coffee was boiling over the fire. Steaks from the hindquarter of a deer Johnny had killed were frying in a skillet. Biscuits were baking in a Dutch oven.

Hal Boyd and Eric came in with three more head. They all squatted around the fire then and ate quickly and with relish. Afterward, they lay around and smoked and finished the coffee.

Tom tilted his hat over his eyes and lay back on the ground. He drowsed. He was awakened by the drum of hoofs against the ground, by Hal Boyd's shout: "Tom! Company!"

He sat up. They were camped in a long, shallow draw. Down the slope from the south galloped ten men, Geier at their head. Geier reined up fifty feet short of the fire, his horse plunging and fighting the bit.

He shouted: "All you men are fired! You're trespassing on Anchor property the same as Tom Otis is. If you drive that bunch of TO cattle another mile, I'll have Yarbo after you for rustling!"

Tom Otis got to his feet, walked slowly and deliberately toward Geier.

He drawled: "You better start for Adams City, then. Because those TO cattle are headed for the railroad at Arnoldsville." He grinned, hoping he showed more assurance than he felt, as he added: "Don't bring Yarbo up here. I owe him something for that knot on my head. I might pay it back if he tries to mess into this."

A few of the men behind Geier began to grin. Tom felt sure that Geier would be able to count on but little support from them. They were Anchor men. While they might not want to risk their jobs by helping Tom Otis, they would still be reluctant to fight him. Geier was looking around, weighing the support he commanded.

His face flushed with anger. He turned back to Tom Otis, his anger fading rapidly. At last he smiled. But the smile was not pleasant. It was dangerous and threatening.

He said: "All right. You win the first hand. I can't stop your roundup now. But I know how long it takes to cover Anchor range. Before you're through, I'll give you a surprise. Keep a man or two on guard, Tom. Sleep light and keep your eyes open. I'll be back."

Without another word and without waiting for Tom to reply, he whirled his horse and dug in his spurs. Tom got a wink or two from Anchor's cowpunchers before they whirled to ride after him.

Tom turned back to the fire. Hal Boyd's face was grave. The others were smiling.

Tom said: "He won't have to go far for a crew that will fight us. We can count on a week. After that, anything can happen."

Hal Boyd nodded. "We'll make the most of that week. Then we'll see."

Tom swung up to his saddle, the others following. Johnny MacIntosh stayed to put out the fire and clean up the camp. The cattle already gathered grazed slowly down the center of the ridge, loose-herded by Jack Lea.

They quit at dark and, bone-weary, ate and flopped beside the fire in their blankets. Two men loose-herded the horses with the cattle. A rope corral at camp held a couple of jingle horses. The watch changed at midnight.

The next day and the several that followed were of the same pattern. Only now they had a man less to work with. Johnny MacIntosh and Lea held the main herd. The other four worked the ridges, nooning in the saddle, bringing their day's gather in to the main camp each night. At the end of a week, they had a hundred and fifty head.

Roundup went on. One by one they cleaned out the finger ridges and moved onto the main plateau. Another week passed. Three hundred head. But now they had to watch. Now they expected attack daily, nightly.

Rations grew short, but neither Tom nor Hal was willing to spare a man long enough to go to town for more. They ate venison, and more venison.

And then, one night, the attack came. With no warning at all, half a dozen men hit the herd an hour after the watch had changed. Shooting, yelling, they stampeded the herd, then whirled to attack the camp.

Tom, only now relieved as guard, was just drowsing off. The first shot brought him wide-awake. The second brought him to his feet. He had built up the fire upon coming into camp, but now he scattered it hastily with a booted foot, stamping out the glowing embers. He could hear the sibilant stir of the camp around him.

A man asked sleepily: "What was that?"

Hal Boyd said sourly: "Geier! He'll be here as soon as he gets them cattle to running. Find yourself a handy tree, boys, and let's give 'em a warm reception."

They waited ten minutes, ten dragging minutes. Tom Otis thought about Jack Lea and Johnny MacIntosh, out there with the herd. He felt a stab of fear for their safety.

Jack might have sense enough to yield to superiority in numbers, but Tom doubted if MacIntosh would show that much judgment. Johnny'd be so damned mad he wouldn't think of anything. He'd see two weeks' hard work melting away and he'd go berserk.

Tom heard another flurry of shots, and a ragged, angry shout. Then they came. Galloping, shouting, they ran over the camp. The night was like pitch.

Hal yelled: "Shoot 'em out of their saddles!"

Tom shot at a looming shape fifteen feet away from him. The horse catapulted forward with a crash. Tom ran past him, fell over the downed rider. He flopped down on the man, found his head by feel, and chopped down with his gun barrel. The man stopped struggling and lay still. A horse lifted directly over Tom as he got up, one hoof tipping his shoulder and sending him sprawling again. Almost in his face a gun flared. Concussion from the muzzle blast set his ears to ringing. He fired at the flash. A man screamed, and a horse ran away riderless.

Somewhere near, Geier's voice was yelling:

"Give it up, damn you! Yarbo's with us! Those of you that resist will hang!"

Tom laughed hoarsely. The sound drew a couple of shots from the brush nearby.

Tom yelled: "Come on in, Yarbo! You, too, Geier! Come on in. You've got to get us before you can hang us."

The mounted attack had failed. Tom had knocked one man from his horse and he could hear the man slinking away through the brush, whimpering about pain in his arm. Another lay unconscious not ten feet from where Tom lay. Hal Boyd had killed one.

A few more shots came, but the raiders were moving away. Raw anger suddenly blazed in Tom. He didn't know how many more were out there. He didn't care. But he knew that every minute of delay meant more time to expend rounding up the scattered cattle.

He roared: "Hal! You and Pete take the jingle horses and see if you can catch a couple more!"

Boyd and Fisk scurried toward the rope corral. A moment later Boyd came back with one of the attackers' horses. A little later, Fisk came back with the other. Tom mounted, and the four rode out, leaving their camp behind, unguarded.

They found Johnny MacIntosh dead, twisted brokenly on the ground, shot in the chest. His horse grazed unconcernedly nearby. Tom wanted to stop long enough to bury him, then remembered what Johnny had died for. He had died to keep the cattle from being scattered. The least those that remained could do for him was to find the cattle again, bunch them. There would be time for Johnny's burial then.

Dawn came crawling up over the rim, gray and cold, gloomy and discouraging. But at least now there was light. The cattle had not run far, but they had scattered, right and left, down into the draws.

Tom, knowing every inch of this range, sent a man alone to each watered draw within a radius of five miles. And he began to hear their shouts almost immediately, the slapping of reins on chaps, their whistles as they urged cattle before them.

Apparently Geier and Yarbo had pulled away to lick their wounds. At noon, Tom tallied two hundred head. At day's end, they had all but a dozen of those that had stampeded.

At their camp, they found what few supplies had remained scattered on the ground. Coffee and sugar and flour. Blankets had been slashed, pack saddles and panniers destroyed. The man Tom had clubbed with his revolver was gone.

He said: "One dead, one wounded, one with a headache. How many were there altogether?"

Jack Lea grunted: "I tallied six. There might have been more than that, but I don't think so."

"Then they've got four left. Three that feel good. I've got a hunch the one I clipped is going to be sick for a day or two."

They buried Johnny MacIntosh and the dead raider, salvaged their cooking utensils and a couple of cups and plates, and went on. In the next week they gathered enough to make a herd of just over four hundred, and went down through the rim into the valley of Elk River. They drove east then, until they reached Arnoldsville and the railroad.

It was here that Tom Otis hit his second snag. Geier had preceded him. Geier and Yarbo. They'd talked to the brand inspector. The man, a slow-moving fellow with a long mustache, met Tom as he drove the cattle into the pens beside the tracks.

"What brand?" he asked.

"TO."

"Thought so." The brand inspector gave Tom a fishy, suspicious glance. "Whose brand is it? What's it registered under?"

Tom, who had been uneasy, began to feel better. His father had insisted that the brand be registered in Tom's own name.

He didn't feel better long. Not when the brand inspector said: "That brand and Anchor brand were foreclosed by the Adams City bank a month ago."

Tom stared at him for a moment. He began

now to see how this had been rigged. Geier had talked to this man. He had arranged to have the cattle tied up here in the pens at Arnoldsville.

He said: "The hell! The bank foreclosed on Anchor. Wasn't nothing said in any of the papers about TO. That's my brand."

The man shrugged. "Can't let you go," he said. "Got to hold you up a while till it gets straightened out." He shifted his cud of tobacco from one cheek to the other and spat.

Tom yanked his gun out of holster and dug it savagely into the man's belly.

If he gave in now, he faced charges of rustling, killing. He'd just as well face charges of intimidating a brand inspector.

He said: "I don't know how much Geier paid you, friend, but you're going to OK this shipment."

The man's breath had been driven from his body by the force of Tom's gun muzzle. His face was pale and he looked sick. His glance would not meet Tom's.

He growled: "And if I don't?"

"I'll kill you."

Tom's voice was almost conversational, yet some quality in it made the man look at him uneasily, and at that moment Tom realized with a shock that he meant exactly what he said. He'd fought the crooked sheriff, Yarbo, in Adams City, he'd been stolen blind by Geier, he'd lost Johnny MacIntosh up on the mesa, and had had his cattle scattered. He'd had enough. Now he'd go whole hog or none. Now, he'd fight.

The brand inspector stared at him for a moment. The blood drained slowly out of his face. His eyes turned flat and scared, and he began to shake.

"You won't get away with this!" he shouted, his voice shrill.

"Maybe not. But you'll pass this herd. Won't you, my friend?"

The man sagged. He nodded dumbly. With Tom following him, he went into the pens and the job of checking brands began.

All were TO. All bore a single brand. When it was done, the brand inspector handed Tom his inspection sheet, signed and approved, and started to go. Tom shook his head.

"Uhn-uh. We'll load 'em first. Then we'll take a little ride back into the hills. When my check clears with the commission house in Denver, we'll come back to town."

By night the cars were loaded. They pulled out behind a slow, puffing engine, heading east. Tom and his crew, herding the brand inspector with them, rode out of town.

After settling upon a place to meet, Tom returned to town. He telegraphed a commission house in Denver, giving instructions that his money was to be mailed to him at Adams City, the sale confirmed by wire to Arnoldsville.

Then he got a room at the hotel and settled down to wait.

VIII

When a day had passed, and another, the marshal of Arnoldsville, a big, slow-witted man in his early thirties, came to see Tom Otis. Tom disclaimed all knowledge of the brand inspector's whereabouts. The marshal didn't believe him, but he went away, grumbling.

Another day passed. On the morning of the fourth day, Tom's visit to the telegraph office got him a thin, yellow envelope. He tore it open, standing on the station platform. It was from the commission house with which Anchor had always dealt. It was dated the day previous and read:

> Cattle all sold. Specie in the amount of $9,147.85 mailed to you Adams City, Colorado, today. Many thanks.

Tom got his horse from the livery stable. In the early morning sunlight, he took the trail out of town that would lead him to his crew's hide-out. By noon, they were on their way home, and a disgruntled brand inspector was on his way back to Arnoldsville, swearing vengeance.

It was near midnight when Tom Otis arrived in Adams City. He went immediately to the hotel with his crew, showed the telegram, and arranged rooms for them all. Then all of them headed for the Colorado Saloon.

There was an odd feeling in the air in town tonight. It was as though something had happened, something of which Tom had no knowledge.

Lily Street was singing as he walked into the Colorado. She spotted him immediately as he came through the door, shortened the chorus of her song, stepped down from the stage, and came toward him. Her face was alight with genuine relief and gladness at seeing him. She was wearing green satin tonight, a gown that sparkled with sequins. A low-cut, daring gown that showed a lot of Lily Street, all of it beautiful.

Tom was conscious that he was trail-dirty, that he needed a shave. He was also conscious of a pleasant, overpowering excitement.

Lily whispered: "Back here. In Mike's office. I've got to talk to you."

With a whispered word to Hal Boyd, Tom followed her down the dim corridor to Mike McGill's office. They went inside, and Tom kicked the door shut behind him. He was remembering Lily's promise: *When you get back, Tom.*

But there was a wide-eyed, frightened look in Lily's face now, and he smiled. How could fright be so inexplicably combined with anticipation? Yet here it was. Lily was afraid of him, yet it was plain that she wanted him to take her in his arms, wanted that desperately.

He crossed the room and took her in his arms. From a frightened woman she turned abruptly into a passionate one. Her arms came up about his neck, her body molded itself to his. Her hands drew his head down and her lips met his.

For this endless moment, there was no Anchor, no Geier, no plan. There was only Lily. Tom's blood became liquid fire, coursing through his body, heating wherever it passed. Her body was soft under his hands, yet there was an unsuspected strength in her.

A dance-hall girl? Perhaps. But Tom knew in this moment that here was more woman than he had ever known before. Here was more woman than he was ever likely to know again. A woman strong of body, strong enough to meet and cope with the harshness of living in a hard and violent land, yet also a woman with a world of woman's softness and gentleness in her.

Her kiss was like drowning. Tom sank down, down, his head reeling, his blood racing and pounding.

His voice was hoarse when he broke away. Lily's lips were parted, and there was something new in her eyes, something he had not seen there before. Defenseless, utterly helpless, she stared at him as if begging him to go on. And he wanted to, more than anything else, but not here. Not in Mike McGill's office.

He said: "The check for the cattle is on its way. It should be here tomorrow. But it was smaller than I had hoped. A little over nine thousand."

Still she looked at him, and suddenly Anchor was no longer important.

There was only one thing in life, and it was this slip of a girl. This girl whose eyes knew too much of life, of men and what drove them. This girl whose eyes had forgotten in this moment all their worldliness, that were now like a schoolgirl's eyes gazing at her first love.

Tom said: "To hell with Anchor! To hell with Geier! All I want is you, Lily. Will you marry me?"

Trouble came to her eyes. Tom turned bitter. "Then revenge is more important to you than anything else?"

Lily was shaking her head. Tears sprang into her eyes. "No, Tom. No! That's not it at all. But I'm not your kind of woman. I'm a dance-hall gal."

Tom laughed harshly. "And I'm a broke cowman. What the hell do I care what you are, Lily? What do I care what you have been? I know how I feel and I know what I want. I want you raising my kids, and keeping my house, and sharing my bed as long as I live. That's what I want, and all the rest of it will be hollow without that."

She came to his arms again then with a little flurry of movement. It was as it had been before. Lily said: "Thank you, Tom."

"Then you'll marry me?"

She nodded, wordless.

Tom began to grin. The grin widened and he began to laugh. From sheer exuberance and happiness.

He said: "Then I'm ready for Geier. There's only one place I know of in this country that's good enough for you, and that's Anchor. I want it back and I'll get it back."

Lily was smiling now, too. "And I'll help you."

"How?"

"It's really rather simple. I've started it already. Tomorrow, Mike McGill and Noah Shults and a few of the other businessmen in Adams City will withdraw their money from Geier's bank. The word's already out."

"What word?"

Lily smiled more broadly. "Why, the word that the bank is insolvent. By ten o'clock tomorrow morning, there'll be a line three blocks long in front of it. And you know, I don't think Geier will have money enough to pay them all."

● ● ●

Tom Otis was up at 7:00. He washed and went downstairs and across the street to the barbershop for a shave.

All evening, after he had left Lily, Tom had sat in the Colorado and listened to talk about the bank. News of a bank's insolvency travels like wildfire. Mike McGill had started the rumor as a favor to Lily. Started it in the Colorado. Noah Shults had started it in the Ute as a favor to Tom Otis.

Cowpunchers and cowmen who were in both saloons carried the rumor out over the country when they left. Already buckboards and buggies were beginning to roll into Adams City. Tom wondered if Geier knew what he was in for yet.

The morning stage rolled into town, and Tom got up out of the barber chair and walked down to the post office. He signed a receipt for his money, counted it, and put it into his pocket. Then he headed for a restaurant.

Everywhere, even at this hour, small groups of men were discussing the bank. Tom ate a hasty breakfast, then took a chair on the hotel verandah. He sat down and watched the growing excitement, a small smile playing across his face.

Geier had had no warning at all. If he'd been in the Colorado last night, he might have known.

Instead, he'd been at Anchor and hadn't got back to town until this morning.

Hal Boyd and the other three cowpunchers who had helped Tom with the TO cattle came out of the hotel, grinned at Tom, and headed for the restaurant. Lily came down, dressed in a demure, red-checked gingham dress, and sat down in a chair beside Tom. She was smiling, and her hand slipped across the space between the two chairs and took Tom's own.

Lilly said: "I gave all my silk dresses away last night. All I've got left are a few like this one." Her glance surveyed him with teasing mockery. "You're hooked, my friend. Now you've *got* to marry me."

Geier came along the street from his two-storied white frame house over at the edge of town. He stared at the line forming before the bank with obvious puzzlement. A shout reached Tom.

"We want our money, Geier! Open up and give it to us!"

Murmurs grew in the street as the man's demand was repeated. Geier smiled and waved his hands expansively.

"Sure . . . sure. Any of you who want your money can have it." But there was doubt in the way he turned into the bank door, doubt and hesitation.

Lily said: "Even if he is honest, even if the

79

bank is as sound as can be, he's still beat. No bank can stand a depositors' run on it. Too much of the bank's money is out on loan."

She got up and went into the Colorado. A moment later she came out with Mike McGill. The two of them began to circulate among the crowd, talking, exhorting, spreading doubt and distrust.

Still Tom did not see how all this would help him to regain Anchor. And he knew Geier, knew the man would fight sooner or later.

Slowly, as the morning progressed, the line before the bank grew. The temper of the crowd began to change. It turned ugly and threatening. Mike and Lily found places in the line and kept talking, fanning the crowd's temper to a fever pitch.

Tom heard Mike shout: "Sure! Everybody in the front of the line'll get their money. But how about them 'way back there? I'll bet you ten to one all they get is a bunch of lousy promises!"

"Promises, hell! We'll have our money, or we'll have Geier's hide!"

And so it went. Tom smiled when he saw Mrs. Wickware and Lucy up at the head of the line.

At 11:00, Geier locked the bank door, leaving Mike McGill and Lily only a few places from it.

Mike shouted: "What did I tell you, friends? You've had it! You're hooked, just like I am.

Geier's got your money, and he'll be leaving town pretty soon!"

The murmurs of the mob rose to roars. "Like hell! He'll decorate a cottonwood limb! Around to the back, boys. Bottle him up! Don't let him get away!"

Sheriff Yarbo came across the street at a shambling run, waving his revolver excitedly.

"Get back! Get back, all of you. I'll have no breaking into the bank. You hear? You hear me?"

Lily started across the street toward Tom. Her glance said—*Now, Tom.*—and he got up. He sauntered toward the bank, shoved his way through the pushing crowd. Yarbo scowled at him.

"Is this your doing?" the lawman demanded.

Tom laughed. He took the money out of his pocket and waved it before Yarbo's face. He said: "There's over nine thousand here. I've got a notion Geier might be interested in seeing me."

IX

Yarbo was scared. His weathered, narrow face was pale, and his hands shook. He tapped the barrel of the gun on the door, and after a moment it was opened a crack

Tom Otis shoved, hard. As the door was flung

open, he whirled, closing it in Yarbo's face and shooting the bolt.

Geier stood beside him. The man was raging, but he was frightened, too. Tom said: "They're beginning to talk about a rope and a cottonwood limb." He grinned at Geier, tasting his victory.

Geier scowled. His right hand rested on the Colt revolver in its holster at his side. He snarled: "Damn you, Otis, you're to blame for this!"

Tom nodded. "Uhn-huh." He riffled the crisp bills in his hand. "But I'm offering you a way out."

"There ain't no way out. The bank's money is all gone."

Tom said: "There's nine thousand here. If you want to take it, I'll go out there and start calming that crowd. This thing can stop as fast as it started if something restores their confidence."

Geier squinted at him suspiciously. Geier would obviously rather have killed him than have asked for an explanation. But he controlled himself with an effort and said: "And what's the price of that nine thousand in cash?"

"Anchor."

"I won't do it! Damn you, I won't do it!"

"Then you'll hang." Tom grinned tightly, dangerously. "Take your pick."

Geier whirled from the door and stalked back

across the lobby toward his office. His neck was brick-red with his fury. His whole body shook with his effort at controlling himself.

At last he said: "All right. Count it out."

Tom shook his head. "Uhn-uh. Suppose you make out a deed for Anchor first. I'll call in Mike McGill for a witness."

For a long moment, Geier hesitated between this and the gun at his side. Finally he sagged. "All right. Bring him in."

He went back to his office, got a deed blank, and began to fill it in. Tom went to the door, opened it a crack, and called for Mike McGill. Yarbo yelled for him, and Mike came forward quickly. He came into the bank, and Tom bolted the door behind him.

Geier signed the deed, scowling blackly, and McGill witnessed it, grinning. Tom counted the money out onto the desk. He stuffed the deed into his pocket.

He felt as though a whole new world had opened up before him, but he knew this was not the end. Geier would not give up this easily. Still, it was enough for now. He went back and opened the door.

He yelled: "I've bought back Anchor! There's plenty of money here now, for all of you!"

The lines formed again. Crowding lines, anxious lines at first. But as time ran on, confidence increased. Tom and Lily and Mike

McGill drifted back and forth through the crowd, talking calmly, instilling confidence.

Noah Shults dropped out of the line, shouting: "Hell, if there's plenty of money. I'm damned if I know what I want mine for!"

That slowed the crowd, made them think. More began to drop out of line. Still others began to form another line to redeposit their money.

Soon the deposit line was longer than the withdrawal line, and not long after that, the withdrawal line was gone. Tom, grinning with irrepressible good humor, relaxed. The bank was saved.

It was not that Tom cared about the bank, or about Geier, either. But if the bank went under, it meant that a lot of people would lose their money. It meant that a lot of people's life's savings would be gone.

He found Lily at the hotel. Unnoticed, the day had slipped away. The sun hung low on the western horizon now.

Tom said: "Come on. You and me are going to the parson's house to get married."

"In this dress?" She laughed happily. "Wait till I change. I won't be a minute."

He grabbed for her, but she eluded him, laughing, and ran into the hotel.

Tom walked across to the Colorado. He thought he'd like to have Mike McGill and Hal Boyd for witnesses. He found them and started them for the parson's house, then went back to the hotel.

Lucy Wickware had been waiting for him in the lobby. She was nervous and ill at ease. She came forward hesitantly, and, when Tom looked at her, he realized that he was not seeing Lucy, but her mother. Her mother was there, in her facial expression, in the compressed set of her lips. He thought: *She's heard that I've got Anchor back.*

Lucy intercepted him and said: "Tom, I'm so glad for you! I'm so glad you've got Anchor back!"

He said gravely: "Thank you, Lucy."

"We'd like to have you for supper, Tom. Mother's baking your favorite pie . . . blueberry."

Tom found it hard to repress a cynical smile, but he managed to do so. He felt sorry for Lucy.

He said: "I'm sorry. I won't be able to make it. I'm getting married this evening."

He could see the hard lines in her face now. They had always been there, but this was the first time he had seen them. Her voice was sharp. "To that . . . to that woman, I suppose. Tom, you're a fool. She's nothing but a . . ."

Tom said: "Lucy!"

Defiantly Lucy cried: "Well, she is! Mother says so. She's only after your money!"

"I wouldn't have Anchor now if it hadn't been for her," he reminded gently.

There was no particular point in discussing this with Lucy. Lucy would never understand. In her own heart, she believed herself to be right, to be a woman unjustly jilted and wronged.

Tom murmured: "Lucy, will you excuse me? I've a lot to do."

He watched her march to the door, back straight and defiant. He felt a fleeting regret that dissipated with his thought: *She'll find someone who suits her better than I ever would.*

He gave her time to walk the block and a half home, then went out onto the hotel verandah.

The sun went down behind the mesa. The orange glow faded from the clouds. Dusk settled down over the town. People moved along the street on their way home for supper. And still Tom waited, impatiently tapping his boot against the porch rail.

The street was almost dark when Lily came out. Tom scrambled to his feet, catching his breath. She was radiantly beautiful, smiling. Silent, adoring him with her eyes, she took his arm and walked down the steps with him. Along the walk they went, past the Colorado.

The parson's house was over at the edge of town right beside the church. Tom felt a sudden chill travel down his spine. He frowned. What the hell was the matter with him? He had the world. He had Anchor, and he had Lily. He had everything he wanted.

It was an animal sense, that chill. An age-old instinct of warning. He tried to explain it away in his mind. He told himself that Geier hadn't the guts to try anything tonight. But he couldn't get rid of the uneasiness, the foreboding. He stopped.

"Lily, go back. Go back to the hotel. Quickly."

She caught his mood instantaneously. Fear widened her dark eyes. Her lips parted, and she wet them with her tongue. Her glance said: *No! No! Not now!*

The shot came from between two buildings. It caught Tom in the fleshy part of his thigh, took his leg out from under him with its force. He collapsed to the walk. Lily bent toward him.

He got to his knees and gave her a vicious shove. Her heel caught in a knothole in the walk and she sprawled into the gutter. The second shot cut the air where she had been standing an instant before.

Tom realized with a sinking feeling that they were entirely exposed. There was no shelter closer than a doorway thirty feet away. Geier, frantic, insane with fury, would shoot Lily, too, because he knew he could hurt Tom by shooting her. There was only one way to protect Lily, then, and that was by exposing himself.

Exerting his will against the pain in his leg, Tom lurched to his feet. His gun was in his hand, hammer thumbed back. The shots had come from across the street. But it was dark there—dark. Tom stumbled off the walk and into the street. The gun, Geier's gun, flashed again. Tom triggered a shot at the flash, but knew it went wide. Glass tinkled as it smashed a window a couple of feet from where Geier stood.

Tom kept on, staggering, swaying. His leg would scarcely support his weight. He could feel the warm blood running down his thigh.

Again that hidden gun flashed. Tom forced himself into a run. Behind him he heard Lily scream.

He reached the far walk and he could see Geier now, could see him as a dark, bulky shape between the two buildings. He lifted his Colt and thumbed back the hammer. He had to stop, or he'd never hit the man. He knew that. His running movement was too lurching, too jerky.

He pulled himself to a halt and shoved the gun out before him. Pain blurred his vision, and he felt nausea and light-headedness. He knew he had but an instant before the walk came up to meet him.

Geier's gun flashed again. Something struck Tom a smashing blow on the shoulder, but it came too late to stop his shot. His gun had flashed even as Geier's bullet hit him. And the shot was right. Tom knew that even as he loosed it.

He felt himself falling, but his eyes were glued

to Geier. The man dropped his gun and his hands flew to his chest, as though to tear that bullet out. They clutched and tore at his coat for an instant, then he pitched forward onto the walk, motionless.

There was a flurry of running steps, of frantic female cries, and then Lily was kneeling beside Tom. A man came running up, and Tom looked at him, grinning.

"Get Doc, quick. I need some patching, and then I'm going to get married."

Lily was laughing, and crying, so he pulled her face down and silenced that with his kiss. Hell, he had the world. He had Anchor and he had Lily, and nothing could take them away from him ever again.

Hang Him High

I

In April, the weather of this high country was uncertain at best. Tonight, rain slanted fiercely out of the north and, as the hour grew late, the solitary rider began to feel the hard sting of sleet.

He knew this country, knew his destination. There was this seemingly endless plateau, brushy where the wind got a sweep at it, timbered on the slopes, in the draws, along the precipitous rims. The ground underfoot was a kind of sandy clay and, as the rain continued, it grew increasingly treacherous until the horse had difficulty keeping his feet under him.

A quick and slender man was Lew Moffit, who rode tonight hunched in his saddle against the storm. He was clad in a tattered slicker that failed to keep him dry, a brush-scarred leather jacket, Levi's, and boots.

A stream of water poured off the brim of his hat in front and a gust of wind occasionally whipped it into his face, which was bony and lean and cast in a pattern both competent and hard. Rain and misery had dampened the reckless light that usually shone from his eyes. In its place it had brought out a bitterness that he usually kept well-concealed. It had brought out something else as well, something almost desperate.

The land ahead—the place on Hangman's Creek—was the last chance for Lew. What happened there would determine the course of his life, would decide if he would live it out like other men or whether he would decorate a scaffold as his father and older brother had done. He had reached that place in the road his life traveled where an unmarked forks had forced him to stop. Now he stood uncertainly at the forks. Along one road lay the things that all men seek. At the end of the other was a hangman's noose.

He halted his horse at the top of the steep shelf trail that wound downward into the valley of Hangman's Creek. He stared into the black void and the symbolism of it did not escape his mind.

He conceded that part of his life's indirection was his own fault. Something in him, some defiance, some contempt for the smug righteousness of the men who had hanged both his father and brother made him seek out the reckless ones, the wild ones, the lawless ones. They had been his companions off and on for the past ten years. He'd had his bad times and his good ones. He had seen two men fall before his gun.

But he had stopped one night last week. He had yanked his horse to a dead and sudden halt in the middle of the road leading into Placerville. Appalled, he had realized that he was riding into town with a gang of outlaws intent on robbing the local bank.

That was the way you drifted when your life had no meaning and no predetermined course. Fortunately he'd stopped himself in time. If he had gone on, it would have been too late. He'd swerved aside and ridden away and the bunch had gone on without him.

From there, his course had led straight here. And he wondered now, as his horse picked its delicate way along the narrow trail, what he would find in the valley below.

It would not be peace—a Moffit would never find peace in the valley of Hangman's Creek. It would not be plenty. Though he owned two sections of land, he had neither cattle nor the money with which to buy them. If the house had not been burned, it was probably wrecked. He would meet hostility every way he turned.

With a burst of unexpected insight never experienced before, he knew one unchangeable thing. For the past ten years he had been running away—from Hangman's Creek and the scaffold that had somehow never stopped haunting his dreams—from the people who had taken his father's and then his brother's life, who had then coldly refused, one after another, to provide a home for the fifteen-year-old they had orphaned. So Lew had run away.

He'd been gone ten years. And now he was back to stay.

Down along the steep, black trail the horse

wound his cautious way. Lew couldn't see a thing, not the ground, or the valley, or even the high rims behind his back. He seemed to be riding in the black, wet sky, suspended by some magic in high mid-air. The only solid things were himself and his daintily walking horse.

The first gnarled, ancient cedar loomed before his eyes at almost the same instant the trail leveled out. Then he was in the midst of them, smelling their fragrance and the sharp, spicy odor of the wet sagebrush that grew in the spaces between.

This pungent odor, more than anything that had happened so far, brought back the sharpness of memory. He hadn't seen either of the two hangings. There had been those who thought he should—see Jess's at least—as a stern lesson to keep him on the straight and narrow as he grew. Those who had objected had won out.

But he'd seen the scaffold afterward as he rode through town. He'd seen it standing like a gaunt, voracious skeleton, an impersonal killer that had taken his family from him and left him alone.

Still downward he went. The bitter cold that had seeped through his wet clothes all the way to his bones began to sting. He discovered that his knees had tremors in them, that his hand trembled as it held the reins.

He gritted his teeth to keep them from chattering. It was only the cold, he told himself. It was only the cold. As soon as he got warm . . .

Down the last, steep pitch he went, the horse sliding wildly in the soggy clay. Horse and man hit the road and the horse went to his knees, throwing the man on ahead to slide to a stop in the muddy road. Cursing softly, Lew got to his feet. He wiped his hands ineffectually on his wet pants.

The horse was up, not hurt, and he remounted. Even wetter and more miserable than before, he continued down the road.

He turned in at the familiar lane, not surprised that no gate barred his passage. Faintly, to right and left, he could see the wreckage of a fence. He had gone no more than a hundred yards down the lane before he spooked up half a dozen head of cattle. They had been standing there miserably, their rumps to the storm. Startled, they trotted toward the willows lining the bank of Hangman's Creek.

Going on, he could hear its roar, a pleasant sound after all these years, a sound that had often lulled him to sleep when he was a boy. The sound brought back other memories, more pleasant ones. Memories of his father, bigger and heavier, but quick like himself, a reckless type of man who acted first and thought later, but one who set a lot of store by his sons and who cherished the memory of his wife.

Memories of his mother, known only through

the tintype of her that had always sat by itself on his father's dresser top, through her clothing stored in the attic that still bore faint traces of her perfume.

The house and outbuildings loomed before him. At least they had not been burned. The house would give him shelter from the storm.

He rode directly to the barn, glad he could not see the ravages of time tonight. The door lay flat on the ground. He went inside and discovered the place was full of cattle that had taken refuge.

He put his horse into a stall and pulled the saddle off. Dry manure was six inches deep on the floor. He slipped the bit out of the horse's mouth but left the bridle on. He tied the reins, then tramped outside again.

Ducking his head against the stinging sleet, he crossed the yard to the house. It was no different here. The door lay flat on the sagging porch.

Inside there was a smell of manure, but no cattle. He fumbled for a match, hoping that it would be dry.

Sound, sudden and unexpected and sharp, made him start violently. "Hyah! Get out of here!"

He found a match but didn't strike it. With a faint grin touching the corners of his mouth he said: "I'm not a cow, lady."

There was silence after that, long silence. At last the voice again, this time touched with fright. "Then who are you? And what are you doing here?"

"Same thing you are, likely. Getting out of the rain. Mind if I strike a match?"

No answer. Lew struck the match against the wall.

He held it aloft. He wanted to see the owner of that voice but his glance didn't get that far. It swept the wreckage of the room and his face mirrored his dismay. This room—it was not the room he remembered at all. Broken furniture, manure, and tin cans littered the floor. The windows were broken out. The wallpaper was stained with rain and spattered with manure.

The match burned his fingers and he dropped it with a startled: "Damn!" He fumbled for another, found, and struck it. He looked toward the staircase from which direction the voice had come.

He could not see her well, nor would he have known that she was a girl except that her voice had told him that.

This match also burned his fingers but not before he spotted a dusty lamp standing on a shelf where cattle couldn't reach. He crossed the room in darkness, fumbled for the lamp, and removed the chimney. Then he carried it to the stairway and put it down on a step.

Her voice again, this time more startled than before: "Lew? Lew Moffit? Is it really you?"

"It's me." He stared toward where she sat halfway up the stairs. He could see her better now, slight but seeming bulkier than she really was because of the ragged patchwork quilt she had wrapped around her shoulders. He recognized the quilt immediately. He had seen it often enough before. It was one his mother had made before he was born.

But he couldn't recognize the girl until she said: "It's Sara, Lew. Sara Kennebeck."

How old had she been when he went away? Nine or ten perhaps. He'd never have known her now even if he had remembered her well.

She said softly: "So you've come back. I wondered if you would."

"I thought maybe everyone had forgotten me by now."

"I hadn't. I thought you'd be coming back someday. Otherwise why would you pay the taxes on this place all these years?"

"How'd you know about that?"

"I inquired at the courthouse whenever I was over at the county seat."

He glanced around the room. He picked up the lamp and started up the stairs. "Isn't there a more comfortable place than this?"

"Yes. Upstairs it's pretty much . . . well, it isn't as bad as this." She got to her feet and walked ahead of him.

He followed her along the hall and into a

bedroom at its end. Rats and mice had been in the bedclothes and had ripped them to shreds. There was a scurrying noise inside the walls.

He stared at the place in dismay. The past ten years had sure as hell taken a heavy toll. It would take months to put this place back in shape.

He put the lamp down on the dresser in the spot where his mother's picture had been. He wondered where it was. He hadn't taken it. The day he'd left he was too upset to think of anything but getting away.

He glanced at Sara and discovered tears in her eyes. She breathed: "It's pretty awful, isn't it?"

He nodded, embarrassed, but also warmed by her sympathy. It was one thing he hadn't expected from anyone on Hangman's Creek.

She asked: "Are you just passing through? Or are you going to sell?"

"Neither." His voice was harsh. "I'm here to stay."

He had not been looking at her as he spoke, but her silence drew his glance. Her expression was contradictory, both dismayed and pleased.

"How . . . ?"

"I don't know. Maybe I can get some money at the bank. First thing I've got to do is rebuild the fence. Once that's done, maybe I can raise a crop of hay." She watched him in silence and after a while he frowned at her. "What are you doing here?"

"I was riding. I got caught in the storm. By the time I got this far I was darned near frozen."

"Doesn't your father worry about you?"

He studied her now, really looked at her for the first time. She was a head shorter than he, slim and straight-standing. The quilt had slipped from her shoulders to which her wet shirt clung. He could see the clean, sharp lines of her throat, the swelling lines of her breasts. She noted the direction of his glance and flushed. She pulled the quilt closer around her but her eyes didn't waver but clung steadily to his.

Her face was delicately formed, the chin strong, the nose straight, the lips full and sweet but uncurved now by any smile. Her eyes seemed to be almost gray in this light and were startlingly beautiful, like the guileless, soft eyes of a newborn fawn. She wore a man's hat, shapeless and soaked, her hair piled under it.

She said in a voice he could scarcely hear: "Father knows I'm safe."

Lew's mouth twisted. "If he knew I was in the country, he wouldn't be so sure."

"Lew, that isn't fair."

"Isn't it? I was pretty upset ten years ago when they hanged Jess. But I wasn't so upset I didn't notice who it was kicking up all the fuss. Your old man wanted to hang Jess from the old cottonwood tree right here in the yard."

"That was ten years ago. He has no reason to hate *you*."

Lew stared coldly into her eyes. "He hates anything that carries the name Moffit and you know he does. If he knew you were here with me . . ."

"You're wrong, Lew. What's past is past. You wait and see."

"I'll wait."

She said: "I'd better go."

He nodded. "Where'd you leave your horse?"

"Under the lean-to out back."

He said: "Come on. Sounds like the rain's about to quit." He picked up the lamp and headed down the hall. She followed silently.

He put the lamp down on the shelf he'd gotten it from and went out into the dripping night.

The rain had almost stopped. A thin cover of melting sleet lay on the muddy ground. He fumbled his way around the house, found Sara's horse, and led him back to the front of the house.

She was standing, silhouetted, in the doorway. He shrugged out of his ragged slicker and handed it to her. "Put this on. It'll help a little and I won't need it tonight anyway."

"Thank you, Lew."

She put the slicker on, took the reins from him, and swung to the back of her horse. She said softly: "Give them a chance, Lew. Just give them a chance."

He didn't reply, and after a moment she turned her horse and rode away. She disappeared into the darkness before she cleared the yard but he waited until the wet, sucking sounds of her horse's hoofs died away.

He went back inside, picked up the lamp, and headed toward the kitchen. If he could get a fire going, maybe he'd dry out enough to get some sleep.

Tomorrow he'd give the town of Kennebeck its chance. But he had no faith in the people here. Around here the name Moffit was a curse. It wasn't likely that ten years or fifty years was going to make much change in that.

II

Through some odd freak of chance, the kitchen door had remained bolted all these years, and, since between kitchen and dining room was a swinging door, no cattle had gotten into the kitchen at all.

A thick layer of dust covered everything. Mice and rats had cleaned the cupboards of everything edible and the containers were either open or shredded on the floor.

Wood filled the wood box beside the stove, just as it had the day Lew Moffit left. He lifted the lid, and with his knife shaved a stick into the firebox. He lighted the shavings, then laid a covering of sticks over them.

The air filled with the odor of scorching dust. He stood close to the stove, letting the heat seep into his chilled body. After a while, the room began to warm and Lew's jacket and soaked pants began to steam.

Partly warmed, he took the lamp again and returned upstairs. Rummaging around, he found some blankets that had not been too badly shredded. He returned to the kitchen, kicked a place clear on the floor, and made a bed there. He lay down and was asleep almost instantly.

Tonight, more than they had been in years, his dreams were tormented by the scaffold again. It loomed above him and he was mounting the steps to it, staring up at the noose swinging lightly in the breeze. Behind the noose, enormous and seeming to float like a cloud in mid-air, was the face of John Kennebeck, twisted with anger and hate as it had been that day he wanted to hang Jess Moffit from the cottonwood right here in the yard of the Moffit Ranch.

Lew grumbled and muttered in his sleep. And the mice stirred in the walls and cupboards.

He awoke at sunrise and got up. He went outside and washed in the creek because the pump refused to work.

Hangman's Creek was high and roiling today, tearing along between its banks with a roaring noise that drowned all other sound. Lew returned to the house, went upstairs, and searched closets and drawers for a change of clothes. He found some of his father's that had escaped the mice, and put them on. He returned downstairs, sat on the front porch steps in the blazing morning sun, and carefully cleaned his gun.

The gun was as symbolic to him as was the scaffold. It was the only protection he had in a country he instinctively felt would be hostile to him.

He stared out at the steaming land. The red-brown shapes of cattle dotted the hay fields, which already were showing the green of new growth. There was much to be done, very little time in which to accomplish it. Part of the fence could no doubt be rebuilt, but much of it would have to be replaced. And if he didn't have it done in less than a month, he just wouldn't get a crop of hay.

He got up and walked to the barn. He saddled his horse and led him outside into the sun. Mud had dried on the horse and his belly was gaunt. Lew swung to his back and headed up the lane toward the road.

An unpleasant kind of tension mounted in him, unpleasant because there was no anticipation in the thought of seeing the town of Kennebeck once more. The scaffold would probably be gone by now. But the town would be the same.

So would the people who inhabited it. Sara Kennebeck was likely the only exception. The others would hate him simply because he bore the Moffit name.

There were no ranches for several miles below the Moffit place. Then there was the Roark place, followed by the McAllister outfit, and after that by Kennebeck's enormous spread. It stretched from a line five miles above the town all the way to the town itself. Haystacks dotted its fields even at this time of year. The buildings sprawled over a full five acres of ground about midway through the place.

The house was of logs, two stories high, and contained, in addition to the living room into which the whole Moffit house would fit, eleven other rooms. Lew had only been inside it once, when he was very small, but he had never forgotten it.

He rode on past. He saw several men moving about the yard down there. He saw one on horseback crossing the field toward the house.

He passed no one on the road, a circumstance that was neither surprising nor unusual. This early everybody was heading toward town, not away from it.

The oddly unpleasant tension he felt increased. His mouth firmed out and his eyes narrowed. He'd be neutral when he rode into Kennebeck. He'd wait and see what the town's attitude was going to be. Perhaps he had been wrong. Why should they hate him just because he bore the Moffit name? He'd been only fifteen when they'd hanged his brother Jess.

There was a low rise just outside of town, bordered on one side by the town dump, on the other by a wide spread of sagebrush and then the creek. He reined his horse to a halt atop this rise and stared.

In ten years, there ought to have been some change, but, if there had, it wasn't visible from here. The town of Kennebeck slumbered in the morning sun, looking exactly as it had looked to him so many times before.

Along the banks of Hangman's Creek, huge cottonwoods towered above the surrounding residences. Eastward, on the rising ground lifting toward the rocky ridge that sheltered the town from that direction, were the business streets, two of them, called Kennebeck Street and First. Kennebeck Street was the more respectable of the two, boasting such establishments as the Cattlemen's Bank, the Antlers Hotel, the Kennebeck Mercantile Company.

First Street was lined with saloons at its upper end, with livery barns, blacksmith shops, saddle makers, gunsmiths at its lower end. It also held the Cottonwood Hotel, smaller and less imposing than the Antlers.

Lew touched his horse's sides with his heels and

rode on toward town, entering it at the northern end of Cottonwood Avenue, which paralleled the winding course of Hangman's Creek.

Shade, dappled by the cottonwoods through which the sunlight filtered, was a pleasant cover for the rain-damp street. Lawns were beginning to turn green. The roar of Hangman's Creek echoed, a steady, penetrating sound. He could hear a hen cackling in a chicken house somewhere nearby, could hear a dog's steady barking, could hear a group of children yelling as they played.

He met no one, and turned at the first inter-section toward Kennebeck Street. He wondered if Jim McGraw still ran the bank and tried to remember what McGraw had been like.

A boy's recollections were made up mostly of impressions, not always reliable. He remembered McGraw for the heavy gold chain that had looped from vest pocket to vest pocket, for the yellowed, gold-mounted tooth that had hung from the chain. He remembered McGraw for his gold-rimmed spectacles that he pinched to his nose when he wanted to read. He remembered him for the magnificent mustache sweeping to right and left of his mouth. But he remembered little else.

He began to pass people on the street, but none of them gave him more than a passing glance, surprising him at first. Then he realized there had been a lot more change in him than there had been in the town.

Unnoticed, he rode on to the bank and halted to swing down from his muddy horse. He looped the reins around the tie rail and hesitated between the bank and the hotel dining room. Perhaps it would pay him to have breakfast and get a shave. No use making a bad impression deliberately. The name Moffit was a big enough obstacle to have to overcome.

He swung right and went past the bank to the hotel several doors down the street. He went first into the hotel barbershop that fronted on Kennebeck Street at the corner of the hotel.

It was empty, so he got into the barber chair. The barber, who Lew did not recognize, flung the cloth over him. Lew said: "Shave."

The man tipped back the chair, turned, and began to prepare lather. He was a small and scrawny man of about forty-five. He began to lather Lew's face. Having done so, he covered it with a steaming towel.

"Stranger in town?"

Lew grunted noncommittally.

"Passin' through?"

Lew grunted again.

"Nice town, Kennebeck. Growing town. Lots of important men livin' here. John Kennebeck for one. Town's named for him. There's talk he'll be the next governor of the state."

Lew didn't even bother to grunt.

The barber removed the towel, lathered him again, and began to shave his jaws. Lew closed his eyes. Sara would have told her father he was back, he thought. Kennebeck would have had time to get over his surprise. He'd have had time to think it over and decide what he was going to do. Lew wondered what that was going to be. He wondered if Kennebeck's hatred of the Moffit name had cooled in the last ten years. He hoped it had. He didn't want to lock horns with Kennebeck. Staying here, making it work out, was going to be tough enough.

The barber finished shaving him and toweled his face. He tipped the chair back up, dried Lew's face, and ran a comb through his hair.

Lew got out of the chair and paid the man. He put on his hat, went through the inside door into the hotel lobby.

There were, perhaps, half a dozen people there. Lew recognized several of them but they obviously did not know him. He crossed the lobby to the dining room and went inside.

It was the same here as it had been in the lobby. Lew sat down and ordered breakfast from the young waitress who came to take his order. He waited patiently in spite of his hunger.

It was strange how his uneasiness, his sense of premonition grew. As though he knew things would not go well. As though he sensed a hostility that did not yet exist, indeed could not exist until the town knew that he was here.

The girl brought his breakfast. Lew ate, trying not to wolf the food. Ravenous, he finished the meal in minutes, drained the coffee cup. One thing he'd have to take back with him whether he took anything else or not. That was provisions.

The girl returned and Lew paid her. He went through the lobby and out into the morning sun. He stood there for a moment while he shaped a cigarette and lighted it.

The tension in him mounted. He'd never been in a bank before for the purpose of asking for a loan. He didn't suppose it was difficult. He had security for the loan in the ranch on Hangman's Creek. He turned and headed for the bank.

The lobby was floored with white tile. The sun, streaming in the big front windows, made it as blinding as snow. There were two tellers' windows, both barred with square brass bars. There was a swinging gate that led toward the rear of the bank.

Lew walked to one of the teller's windows, waited until a woman in front of him had finished, then said: "I want to see about a loan."

The teller's eyes met his, then immediately shifted away. He said: "Yes, sir. Just go through that gate over there. Mister McGraw will take care of you."

Lew nodded. It was easier than he had expected. He had thought the teller would question him, a little bit at least, before letting him see McGraw. So far as the teller knew he was a stranger and for a stranger to seek a loan . . . Unless the teller knew who he was. But how could that be unless Kennebeck had been here earlier today?

He put the thought away from him. He left the cage and went to the gate. He pushed it open and walked back to McGraw's desk.

McGraw saw him and stood up. He hadn't changed, Lew thought. The same ponderous gold chain spread across his vest, supporting the same gold-mounted, yellowed tooth. He still wore the magnificent mustache, though now it was touched with gray. His glasses were pinched to his nose and he peered through them near-sightedly. "Yes?"

His manner indicated that he failed to recognize Lew. But his eyes gave that the lie. Because they did, sudden, irrational anger rose in Lew. "You know me, McGraw. Kennebeck told you I'd be in."

The eyes behind the gold-rimmed glasses sharpened. He said briskly: "Yes, Moffit. I know you. Kennebeck said you would be in. Now what can I do for you?"

"I need a loan. I'm back to stay, but, if I expect to make a living, I've got to repair and rebuild

113

the fence. If I do that, I can still get a crop of hay this year."

McGraw didn't immediately reply. When he did, it was to say: "I should think your memories of Kennebeck would be too unpleasant for you to want to come back and stay. Why don't you sell out? Mister Kennebeck has authorized me to . . ."

"Never mind. I'm not going to sell. Do I get the loan? Two hundred dollars ought to make a pretty substantial start. When that's gone, you can come see what I've done with it, and, if you're satisfied, then lend me enough to finish up the job."

McGraw was shaking his head. Lew guessed he had expected this all along, yet the unreasonableness of it made his anger increase. They didn't want him here. They figured if they refused him the chance to make a go of it, he'd sell out and leave the country for good.

He said furiously: "Kennebeck tells you . . . !"

McGraw nodded. "Sure. He owns a healthy slice of the bank and he tells me what to do. He tells everybody in the country what to do. He's telling you to sell out and go before it's too late."

Lew shrugged. There was a strange kind of hostility in McGraw's near-sighted eyes, but there was something else as well, resentment, perhaps a sneaking sympathy that was in sharp contrast to the hostility. McGraw said: "Good day, Moffit. If at any time you should want me to handle the sale of your property for you . . ."

Lew growled: "If I do, I'll let you know."

He went out angrily and stood, smoldering, on the walk before the bank. Damn Kennebeck anyway! There was apparently no end to the man's hate, no limit to his vindictiveness.

He fished tobacco from his pocket and shaped himself a smoke. He puffed it thoughtfully. He had $14 to his name. Enough, perhaps, to buy provisions enough to last a couple of months. But no more than that. There was nothing for wire or staples, no overflow for repairing the fence or even for fixing the windows of the house.

His eyes smoldered and his jaw firmed out. They weren't going to beat him out this easily. If he couldn't buy materials to fix the fence, he'd fix it with what was left of the old fence. He'd board up the windows of the house. He'd put up a crop of hay somehow, and after that . . .

He turned his head and saw Kennebeck coming toward him from the direction of the hotel. The man halted in front of him, a toothpick between his colorless lips. "You must be Lew Moffit."

Lew nodded. Hostility had risen in him, and unreasoning anger.

Kennebeck was a big man, broad-shouldered, slim-hipped, running to a bit of a paunch these days. He wore his hair long, like the mane of a lion, but, like McGraw's mustache, it was touched with gray. Lines were visible in Kennebeck's face that had not been there ten years ago. But his eyes and mouth were the same, cold and thin and hard.

Lew said: "You told McGraw to turn me down."

"Why, yes, I did. I wanted to talk to you. Come on to the saloon with me. I'll buy you a drink while we talk." Being civil was plainly a strain on Kennebeck.

Suspicion touched Lew. He opened his mouth to refuse, then closed it with a snap. It would do no good, but neither would it do any harm to find out what Kennebeck had on his mind.

III

Kennebeck moved away downstreet and Lew swung along beside him, his suspicion mounting. The man seemed in no mood to talk. Scowling and taciturn, he kept his face straight ahead and walked swiftly. Lew had to hurry to keep up and the fact that he was willing to do so made him angry at himself. If there was hating to be done, he was the one with justification for it. Kennebeck had no call to hate. Not any more. Whatever reasons he had possessed for hating the Moffit clan had been wiped out on the

116

scaffold, here in the town of Kennebeck more than ten years ago.

Lew glanced angrily aside at the rock-hard face. Those eyes were as cold as ice, he thought. How the hell did a man like this raise a daughter like Sara?

So engrossed was he with his thoughts that he paid no attention to where they were. When he finally did notice, Kennebeck was swinging around a corner at the lower end of town. The older man headed for First. Ahead, Lew could see the towering old yellow frame building that housed the McClannahan Livery barn.

He said: "Where the hell are you taking me? There's no saloon down here."

Kennebeck swung his head. His eyes narrowed, small and cold, and seemed to chill Lew with their glance. A cold core of fury began to form in Lew's mind.

He began to feel uneasy. He ought to stop, he thought. Nothing had changed for Kennebeck. His hatred of everything that bore the Moffit name still lived. Telling McGraw to refuse the loan proved it. Kennebeck's hatred wouldn't die until the last of the Moffit clan was dead.

Lew's uneasiness grew until it crowded all else from his mind. It was a vague thing, without firm basis in any tangible fear. He wasn't afraid of Kennebeck, he told himself. He'd meet the man anytime, any place, with any weapon or with no weapon at all. What, then, did he fear? What was it about this end of town that made his stomach churn?

He knew—he understood both his own uneasiness and Kennebeck's plan when they turned the corner onto First. For there it was, unchanged except that it was weathered by the years, by the winter storms and summer sun. The scaffold. The one he had been so sure would have been torn down by now. It stood there in the same place it had stood so many years before.

Here Lew's father had died. Here his brother Jess had also died less than a year later. This was the scaffold that had haunted his dreams all the ten years he had been away.

He stopped dead in his tracks. Kennebeck went on half a dozen steps, then stopped and swung around. Lew said in deliberate and measured tones: "You dirty son-of-a-bitch!"

Kennebeck's eyes were still narrowed and hard. But his thinned-out mouth had a cruelly triumphant grin written on it. He said: "Take a look at it. Take a damned good look. It's waiting for you. It's been waiting all these years."

Lew's lips scarcely moved. His blood seemed to have turned to ice. He stared at Kennebeck, but a part of his glance couldn't help taking in the scaffold beyond. "I ought to kill you!"

Kennebeck's lips twisted. "That's one way of getting there."

"You bastard! You rotten bastard!"

"That's the kind of talk I'd expect from you."

Lew wanted to kill him. He had never wanted anything more in his life. He glared at Kennebeck, his muscles tense, teetering in this moment on the very edge of rashness and violence. Whatever he did, it would be wrong.

Kennebeck said: "I'll tell you something else. I'll tell you just one time. Stay away from my girl."

"Stay away from her? You damned old fool, I didn't look her up."

A kind of insane wildness flared in Kennebeck's eyes. It was hate, more virulent than anything Lew had ever seen before. Amazement touched him, and fear, and then both emotions were driven away by another— doubt—and a dawning suspicion so terrible that it momentarily horrified him.

He'd been fifteen when Jess was hanged, even younger when his father was executed. Out of loyalty he had stoutly refused to admit that either of them had been guilty of the crimes of which they had been accused. But deep inside he had never doubted that they were guilty. A whole town said they were. A jury said they were. A judge had sentenced them both to hang.

Now, in this instant, he really doubted for the first time. So virulent, so bitter, so terrible was Kennebeck's hatred that Lew suddenly knew he would do anything—perjure himself—even plan incriminating circumstances to ensure satisfaction of his hate. But why? For God's sake, why? It was something he'd find out. And soon.

Kennebeck screeched: "You belong on that scaffold, too! The town wanted to tear it down but I wouldn't let them. I knew you'd be coming back, so I kept it here, waiting for you. Look at it, Moffit! Look at it good. Your old man danced a jig on the end of a rope up there and so did your brother Jess. I watched 'em. I watched their bodies twitch and jerk and I watched their faces turn blue. . . ."

Suddenly Lew could stand no more. Something—some rein of control snapped almost audibly in his mind.

Before he quite realized what he was doing, he lunged forward, face contorted, eyes blazing with fury and outrage. His fist slammed squarely into John Kennebeck's mouth.

Lips and teeth gave before its force. Arms windmilling, blows raining in Kennebeck's face, he drove the man back, trying with his frantic blows to crush the ugly look of ghoulish pleasure from Kennebeck's face. He saw nothing, was aware of nothing but the man and the terrible compulsion he felt to smash him as he might smash some poisonous reptile.

He didn't see the men moving upon him from

three sides. He didn't know they were there until he felt their hands, felt their hard and bony fists pounding him as he had pounded John Kennebeck, bruising, cutting, stunning him with their repetitious force.

He heard their voices, the curses, the obscenities they heaped on him. He fought as he had never fought before, across the street, down in the dirt half a dozen times before he reached the scaffold on the other side. A man bawled: "Hang him! Hang the dirty son-of-a-bitch!"

Lew went down again. Kicks struck him in the ribs, in the chest, high on the left cheek bone. He fought to his feet, nearly unconscious and going purely on nerve. He backed to the scaffold steps, his eyes blazing, his mouth an ugly slash in his dirty, bloody face. With the scaffold steps at his back, he kicked out savagely, catching one man in the throat and sending him reeling back into the others, choking and gasping as though he were near to death.

It was hot sun, and blood, and dust and pain. But now it was mostly pain. His chest felt as though it had been caved in. His ribs felt as though half of them were broken and sticking through his skin. The muscles of his legs and arms had knotted against the pain of the kicks they had absorbed.

A voice howled: "I got the rope! I got the rope! Now drive the bastard to the top!"

A thrown rock struck Lew on the forehead. The world, the street filled with hating, lusting men turned red, then gray, then black. Desperately he clung to the scaffold rails, unable for the moment even to raise his feet to kick them away.

It was the end, he knew. He had come three hundred miles for this—not the things that men seek for themselves, family, friends, a secure place in which to live and work. He had taken the wrong turn in the road, had taken the one that led straight to a hangman's noose.

Helpless, he could fight them off no more. They were too many and he was too badly beaten. In seconds they would swarm over him, drag him to the top of the scaffold, and put the rope around his neck. The trap would drop and he'd fall until the rope caught his body and suspended it in mid-air. As his father and Jess had done, he would kick out the last sparks of life before the lusting, gloating eyes of the men who hated him.

Dimly he saw them, dimly felt them coming. He felt their hands seize him and drag him toward the top. He fought for consciousness. At least he could die like a man, like a Moffit. He could spit in their faces before they sprang the trap.

Fighting thus for consciousness, he only dimly heard the discharge of the shotgun, only dimly heard the roaring voice: "Stop! Next barrel will get at least a dozen of you! Turn him loose and get down off of there!"

He heard the thundering voice, but nothing changed. He was dragged to the top and held while fumbling hands placed the noose over his head and drew it tight on his neck. The ponderous hangman's knot was harsh and hard against the left side of his head as the rope snapped tight.

He heard the shotgun roar again and this time heard the rain of shot striking the ancient timbers of the scaffold.

Howls of pain broke from a dozen throats at once. The hands holding Lew relaxed and dropped away. Men jumped from the scaffold and tumbled down its steps.

He turned his head, focused his eyes on the blurred figure standing out there in the street alone. Whoever it was had the gun broken and was punching fresh shells into the breech. Lew caught a gleam of sunlight against the star the man wore on his vest.

With stunned amazement, Lew realized he was alone. He stood by himself at the top of the scaffold, the rope around his neck.

He was standing on the trap. Instinctively, as he realized this, he stepped aside to the edge of it. He raised his hands to remove the noose.

The trap sprang with a crash. Lew grabbed for the rail, caught it, and clung there, shaking from head to foot. Someone had thrown the trap. Someone hated him enough to take that chance, even in the face of the marshal's gun.

He clung to the rail for a moment until his shattered nerves steadied. Then he raised his hands again, standing as tall as he could to take the strain off the rope.

He removed the noose and released it. He grabbed the rail again and moved cautiously to the steps. He went down, almost falling twice, and reached the bottom with his knees shaking so badly he could scarcely stand.

He sat down on the second step. He leaned forward to let his head hang between his knees.

He hadn't been very smart. He should have stayed with the wild bunch and ridden into Placerville. Perhaps a noose did wait at the end of that road, but there was a noose at the end of this one, too. And this road looked as though it was going to be mighty damned short.

Slowly his consciousness sharpened as blood ran into his head. With its return came a sharpening of the pain. There was not an inch of him that didn't ache or throb or burn.

Dimly he heard the marshal's roaring voice as he cleared the street. Who had all the men been who had taken over Kennebeck's dirty work? Kennebeck's ranch hands, he supposed. Maybe a few of Kennebeck's friends from the town.

It had not been spontaneous, this thing that had

happened to him. It had all been very carefully planned. Kennebeck had offered him a drink, reasonably sure it would not be refused because Lew Moffit would know he had enough trouble without inviting more.

With sharp and deliberate cruelty, Kennebeck had led him to the lower end of town, to the scaffold where his father and brother had died. When the mere sight of it failed to make Lew fight, Kennebeck had taunted him. Then his men, certainly not there by accident, had taken over for him.

A monstrous thing, one that increased Lew's doubt of his father's and brother's guilt until it was almost certainty.

He heard the marshal's steps and glanced up, his eyes hard and very determined now. He'd stay on at Hangman's Creek. He'd stay, and before he was through, he would have the truth. He would clear his father's and brother's names or he would die himself.

The marshal was of about the same size as Lew, but older. Lew guessed his age at about forty.

Something of a dandy, the man was dressed in fawn-colored trousers, carefully creased, boots that gleamed in the sun, a wool shirt that fitted his deep chest and heavily muscled shoulders tightly. He must have come from his office too hastily to grab his hat, for his head was bare.

He said: "So you're Lew Moffit."

Lew nodded. The marshal must have come to town in the past ten years because he didn't know Lew.

"And living up to your family name already, looks like."

Lew stood up. There was suddenly a dangerous glint in his eyes. "Are you saying this was all my fault?"

"Wasn't it?"

Lew said: "Marshal, Kennebeck laid a trap for me. Seems like any damned fool could see that with his eyes shut. He invited me for a drink after the banker turned me down on a lousy two-hundred-dollar loan because Kennebeck told him to. I accepted. Maybe it was stupid, but I didn't see why Kennebeck should hate me. Only he didn't head for any damned saloon. He brought me here. He threw that scaffold in my face and even described in detail the way my father and brother died. I jumped him, Marshal. I jumped him good and I'd do the same damned thing again. Only he had it all rigged. He had his crew waiting. So if you're looking for someone to pin the blame on, look for Kennebeck."

"Going to fight everyone that mentions it?"

"Maybe. If they throw it at me the way Kennebeck did."

"And maybe you'll end up there yourself."

"Maybe I will." Lew's anger was rising now. He knew he owed the marshal his life but it didn't seem to help. "And maybe I'll do something else while I'm still around. Maybe I'll find out if my father and brother did the things this town hanged them for."

"You think there's any doubt?"

"I think there's one hell of a lot of doubt! When Kennebeck hates, he doesn't draw any lines. You saw that for yourself a few minutes ago. If he'd see me hang for punching him in his lying mouth, what makes you think he wouldn't see my father and brother hang just because he hated them?"

"Better cool off, youngster. Better go home and cool off."

Lew glared at him. "I'll go home, but I won't cool off."

"I won't always be around. . . ."

Lew said: "You won't have to be. Next time I'll be on guard. It won't be me that gets hurt next time. It'll be Kennebeck and his crowd."

He started to walk away. His right leg gave and he almost fell. The marshal caught his arm. "Come on uptown and see Doc first. Let him patch you up."

"The hell with that. I haven't got money to waste on doctor bills. What I've got has got to last."

The marshal grinned at him, his eyes not quite

127

so hard as they had been before. "I'll tell Doc to send the bill to Kennebeck."

Lew stared at him. There was a certain sympathy for him in the lawman's eyes. But he was under no illusions as to where the marshal would stand when the showdown came. This was Kennebeck's town, named after him and owned by him. On important matters, the people did what Kennebeck told them to.

IV

Lew Moffit limped uptown at the marshal's side. As they walked, the fury in him faded, to be replaced by horror at what had so nearly happened to him. The fact that he had escaped death by hanging was in itself miraculous, dependent upon small and inconsequential things. If the marshal had not arrived at the precise instant he had . . . if he had not been the kind of man he was . . . if Lew had not stepped off the trap exactly when he had . . .

He turned his head. "How long have you been in Kennebeck?"

"Five, six years."

"Been marshal all that time?"

"Uhn-huh. Name's Weller. Court Weller."

The doctor's office was upstairs over the Kennebeck Mercantile Company. Lew climbed the stairs painfully and the marshal followed.

He opened the door at the head of the stairs, went along the hall, and entered the office upon the door of which was painted: HERBERT S. MILES, M.D.

The waiting room was empty. From an adjoining room, he heard Doc Miles yell: "Be with you in a minute! Take a seat."

He remembered Doc's voice and suddenly remembered the man himself. But he didn't sit down. He walked to the window and stared down, into the street.

After several moments the door to the adjoining room opened and Doc stood framed in it. There was no immediate recognition in his eyes. Weller said: "This here's Lew Moffit, Doc. And this is Kennebeck's work. Fix him up and send the bill to Kennebeck."

Doc peered at Lew. "It is you, isn't it? You back to stay?"

Doc was a stocky, untidy man who looked more like a blacksmith than a doctor. He wore a Vandyke beard, probably to give him a professional look, and gold-rimmed spectacles. His hands were big, broad, and powerful. His forehead was bony and high, his brows heavy, his jaw bones prominent and as strong as his corded neck beneath.

Lew nodded. "I'm back to stay."

Doc said: "I wouldn't, if I were you. I'd

leave while I could. You won't last a month on Hangman's Creek."

Lew didn't answer.

Weller said: "He's right, Moffit. You can't buck Kennebeck. He'll . . ."

Lew stared at him. "He'll what? Do anything to get rid of me? Even rig up something and get me hanged legally? I'm getting curious, Weller. If he'll fix up a welcome home party like that one down on First Street for me, maybe he's got a reason for wanting to be rid of me. Like something he doesn't want known. Like maybe that the two Moffits who were hanged before weren't even guilty of the things they were supposed to have done."

"They had a proper trial."

Lew stared at him sourly. "You don't believe that and neither do I. Kennebeck was as strong then as he is right now. First thing I'm going to do when I get my place straightened out is ride over to the county seat. I'm going to find out some things . . . who the men on my father's and brother's juries were and what they owed Kennebeck to make them do just what he told them to."

It was a rash accusation and he knew it. So far he hadn't anything to go on but an uneasy feeling that both trials ought to be investigated.

Weller said: "Keep poking around and you're liable to end up dead."

Doc Miles snapped irritably: "How the hell am I going to patch you up if you're going to stand here jawing all day long?"

Lew wanted to probe Weller's statement further, but he shrugged and followed Doc into the inner office. He took off his shirt and sat down.

He heard the outer door close, afterward heard Weller's steps faintly on the outside stairs. The pungent, sharp odor of alcohol filled his nostrils as Doc began to sponge off the abrasions on his face and upper body.

He asked: "What kind of a man is Weller, Doc?"

Doc didn't reply immediately. At last he said: "Good enough. He keeps the peace. He doesn't belong to Kennebeck, but he knows Kennebeck can get rid of him. You can't count on him, Lew. He helped you today, but he won't be able to help you at all outside the limits of the town. That's the sheriff's job and the sheriff is twenty miles away."

Lew said: "I'll grow eyes in the back of my head."

"You might need 'em, too. Now shut up and let me finish you."

Ten minutes later, Lew shrugged into his dirty, bloody shirt. He thanked Doc Miles and went outside. He clumped painfully down the steps, stood while he shaped a smoke from the crushed sack and rumpled papers. With it dangling from his mouth, he got his horse and led him to the front of the Kennebeck Mercantile Company.

He tied the horse and went inside. From a young man he had never seen before he bought the supplies he thought he would need during the next couple of weeks. In addition, he bought staples, wire cutters, and a hammer.

He dumped everything into a gunny sack, carried it out, and tied it behind his saddle. He still had $7 left. He mounted and rode slowly out of town.

He was stiff and sore and every movement of the horse hurt. Doc had cleaned the dirt from the abrasions, put liniment on the bruises, and had ascertained that there were no broken bones. But he hadn't helped the pain.

Lew rode cautiously until he reached Kennebeck's upper fence line, but nothing happened. Thereafter he relaxed, and in his mind faced the mountainous task confronting him.

He would work harder in the next few months than he had ever worked in his life. Several miles of fence must be repaired, made strong enough to keep cattle out of the hay fields. The house must at least be made livable. And, later in the summer, several hundred tons of hay must be cut and raked and stacked.

All this might have been possible under normal

circumstances. Any place but here, he'd have been able to borrow what money he needed, using the ranch as security for the loan. He'd have been able to count on the help of neighbors and townspeople in putting up the hay.

But not here. Not with Kennebeck aligned against him. Not with Kennebeck willing to do anything to see him hanged.

He reached home, unsaddled his horse, and picketed the animal out in the hay field to graze. He limped to the house and stood before it, staring with discouragement.

Slowly, as he stared, his anger began to stir. To hell with Kennebeck! The man wasn't going to drive him away. He wasn't going to be defeated, either. There was a weak spot in Kennebeck's armor some place. All he had to do was find it.

Today he'd clean out the house and fix the doors. Tomorrow . . . well, the fence would have to wait. There was no use trying to fix it until he got Kennebeck off his back. One of Kennebeck's men could destroy, each night, what Lew had labored all day to build.

Tomorrow, then, he'd ride to Glen Cañon, the county seat. He'd examine the records of his father's and brother's trials. Maybe by tomorrow night he'd have some ammunition with which to fight.

The task of cleaning up the house seemed mountainous. He started upstairs, first carrying out everything that could not be repaired and piling it in the yard for a huge bonfire. Then he swept. After that, he spread poison wheat, which he had bought in town, on the floors to kill the rats and mice.

Downstairs was worse, but he kept working steadily all through the day. He shoveled manure and trash out of the living room. He got boards from the outbuildings and boarded up the windows. He swept, and scrubbed, and re-hung the door and fixed the lock on it. Sundown caught him by surprise with still much to be done, but with much accomplished, too.

He stopped and, carrying towel and soap, went down to Hangman's Creek where he stripped off all his clothes. He bathed in the icy water, dressed himself, and returned to the house.

Activity had relieved some of the aches Kennebeck's beating had left with him. He built up the fire in the kitchen stove, stirred up some biscuits, and put bacon on to fry.

Kennebeck wouldn't let him alone. He was sure of that. Kennebeck would bring the fight to him, perhaps tonight, perhaps tomorrow. There was but one defense against a man like Kennebeck. That was to attack, and attack again, and keep attacking until the fight was won.

He finished his supper, heated water on the stove, and washed the dishes. He went outside and sat on the porch, smoking, staring into the dark and silent night.

Hoof beats coming down the lane brought him to his feet and sent him silently to the corner of the house, gun in hand, hammer back.

The horse pulled up before the porch. Lew waited silently, puzzled that there was only one rider, wondering where the others were. At last he called: "All right. Tell me what you want and then get the hell out of here!"

He heard a nervous laugh, then Sara Kennebeck's voice: "Lew! Are you all right? I just heard . . ."

Lew holstered his gun and walked to where she sat her horse. He said harshly: "I'm still alive but I wouldn't be if Weller hadn't butted in."

"I'm sorry, Lew. I didn't think Father . . . I told him you were back, but I didn't know he'd try to kill you."

"You told him I was going to borrow money from the bank, too, I suppose."

"Yes." She swung down off her horse and stood there in the darkness without moving. "You were right, Lew, and I was wrong. I'm sorry. I'll do anything I can. . . ."

"There's nothing you can do. It's already been done."

"Lew, please, aren't you even going to invite me in?"

"All right. Come in." His tone was sour.

Tonight the name Kennebeck was a dirty word to him.

He led the way into the house and lighted a lamp.

Sara's eyes clung to him steadily, tears brightening them as she saw the marks her father and his men had put on him. She said: "I didn't know it would be like this. If I'd just kept still . . ."

"Forget it. I guess we don't choose our parents or control the things they do, either."

"But why did he do it? Why? You never did anything to him. You were only fifteen years old when you left here."

"He's been saving that scaffold for me. He knew I'd come back someday."

"But why?"

"I don't know, but I'm going to find out, if I can. Tomorrow I'm going over to Glen Cañon and have a look at the trial records. There's no use doing anything around here until I know your father's going to stay off my back. And the best way I know to get someone to let me alone is to hit them before they get a chance to hit me." He scowled at her. "Are you going to tell him that, too?"

She flinched. "Lew, you're not being fair. I told him last night, but I didn't know what he'd do. I won't give you away again."

"All right. You want some coffee?"

She nodded. He picked up the lamp and headed for the kitchen with Sara following. She said: "I can see you've been working today. It looks real nice."

"Thanks."

He set the lamp down in the kitchen, got a couple of cups, and poured them full. It occurred to him that if Kennebeck knew she was here— good God, the man would burn the place to the ground and Lew with it. Hating Lew as he did, the thought of his daughter and Lew . . .

He studied Sara in the light of the lamp between them on the table. She was even prettier than he had thought she was last night. Her hair, instead of being tucked under a shapeless man's hat, framed her face and was drawn into a bun on the nape of her neck. It seemed almost reddish in the light of the lamp, but he knew that was an illusion. Actually it was a golden color, like fresh-threshed straw in the fall sunlight.

And her eyes—they seemed bluer than they had last night, and less gray. Her mouth was full and soft and the lower lip seemed inclined to tremble slightly. He wondered what it would be like to kiss that mouth and secretly decided to find out soon.

He sipped the scalding coffee, watching Sara as he did. She held her cup in both small hands, raising it occasionally to sip its contents. When she did, her eyes would meet his over the rim of the cup, and every time that happened, her color heightened.

The things only partly concealed in a woman's eyes—these things are not obscure to a man and were not to Lew. He looked away from her and said almost angrily: "Why do you bother to be nice to me? It'll get you in trouble if you keep it up. Best thing you can do is stay the hell away from me. Don't come back here again. I'm going to tangle with your father, and, when I do, only one of us is going to come out of it alive. Either way, you're going to get hurt."

She was silent for a long time. When he glanced at her, he saw that she was close to tears. He asked: "What did I say?"

"It's nothing you said. You couldn't know."

"Know what?"

"That I've been waiting for you to come back just as much as Father has. For a different reason."

"Hell, I hardly knew you." He felt trapped and angry.

"But I knew you. I used to dream that you and I . . ." She stopped, avoiding his eyes.

"Of all the damned fool things! You know what I am. I'm a Moffit. There isn't a man in the country that would put up even money I'd last a month. You can find yourself someone with a better chance than that."

"I don't want someone else." There was a

138

stubborn set to her mouth. He got up and reached impatiently for her coffee cup. She caught his hand and pulled herself to her feet. Her arms went around his neck and her mouth raised itself to his.

Lew didn't like the thoughts that were going around in his head. Angry thoughts of revenge against Kennebeck. He wanted to hurt Kennebeck as badly as Kennebeck had hurt him. And he was thinking that Sara was made to order for it.

He lowered his mouth to hers and kissed her— savagely—almost brutally. His arms tightened around her, bringing her body hard against his own.

He could feel her trembling, but could detect no withdrawal. He picked her up and carried her to the door, limping slightly under her added weight. He opened the door and carried her out into the spring night.

Here in the darkness he couldn't see her face, nor she his. He could do what he wished with her. He could get on with his revenge.

Down toward the creek he carried her and no protest came from her lips. Her arms were around his neck, partially supporting her weight. Her body continued to tremble.

He put her down in a patch of soft grass beside the creek. He lay down on the ground beside her.

He found her mouth and kissed her again, as

savagely as before. She returned his kiss, with no words before or after it.

Almost angrily he made love to her, and, when he was finished knew a shame, a disgust with himself he had never experienced before.

He cursed softly and tried to see her face in the faint starlight. All he could see was the shine of her eyes, a brightness that had to be tears.

She had given herself willingly, out of love for him. He had taken her out of anger and desire for revenge.

He was exactly what Kennebeck thought he was, and perhaps it would have been better if Kennebeck had succeeded in hanging him today.

V

About to utter an apology to her, Lew Moffit suddenly stopped himself. She lay beside him on the grass, still and silent, staring up at the stars. He had begun this out of a burning need to avenge himself. Now, surprisingly, he was feeling something else.

He had never known a girl like Sara. He sat up suddenly and his jaw clenched hard. He said, his voice very harsh: "I've got to tell you something about Lew Moffit. When I'm finished, I don't think you'll like me much better than I like myself."

She didn't speak, and he hadn't expected her to. He went on: "Up there at the house . . . before we came down here . . . all I was thinking about was how much I could hurt your father through you."

Her voice was very small against the roar of the creek. "I knew that, Lew."

"And you let me . . . ?"

Now he wished he could see her face. He stared at her, trying to make out her expression, failing because of the lack of light. He said, less harshly than before: "But something happened. I . . . I don't want you now because it will hurt John Kennebeck. I want you . . . to be with me all the rest of my life, whether it's here or some place else."

A sound, almost a sob, escaped her throat. He turned to her and gathered her gently in his arms. Her body shook, and the strength of her arms had a quality of desperation.

He said: "When I came back, I was looking for something to hold on to. I thought this place was it. But the place doesn't matter any more. Not if you'll come with me and marry me."

"He wouldn't let us, Lew. You know he wouldn't. He'd follow and kill you or have you killed."

"Why? For God's sake why? What's he got against me? Just that I belong to the Moffit family?"

"It has to be more than that. I think he's a little insane where the Moffit family is concerned. It probably began before either of us was born. And the hangings made it worse because he can't forgive himself for them."

"You don't think . . . ?"

"I think that Father perjured himself to get your father and brother convicted. I think he believes he will be rid of his guilt over doing so only when you are dead."

Lew said soberly: "If I stay, I'll eventually have to fight him. And one of us will die."

Again her voice was so small he could scarcely hear it over the roar of the stream. "I know that, Lew. But it's the only way. If we run, he'll have another reason for hating you. Neither of us will know when it's coming, but we'll both know it is."

"I suppose you're right." He was tired, suddenly, tired from the day, from the beating he had taken that morning.

Sara murmured: "I'd better go on home, but I don't want to, Lew. I'm afraid to go. I'm afraid something will happen to you while I'm gone."

He squeezed her reassuringly. He grinned. "If you stay, something sure as hell will happen. He knows you were here last night. It's the first place he'll look for you. Not that I give a damn. I'd as soon get it over with."

"No. I don't want it to happen yet. I'll go."

He walked her up to the house, kissed her, and boosted her onto her horse. She sat there for a moment, and said at last: "You won't change, Lew? You don't think . . . ?"

"I won't change."

She turned her horse and trotted him up the lane. Lew stood there in the darkness, motionless, until the hoof beats died away, leaving only the roar of Hangman's Creek tearing along between its banks.

Much had happened in the past twenty-four hours, he thought. The lines had been drawn and the conflict between Kennebeck and him begun. That he was even alive tonight was a miracle in itself.

Sara. He thought of her and repeated her name to himself. Could a man fall in love in twenty-four hours? He hadn't thought so until now. But when he thought of losing her—of perhaps never seeing her again—the ache in his chest became intolerable, and a reckless wildness came to his brain.

He'd ride to Glen Cañon tomorrow. He'd look at the records of the trials of his father and brother so many years ago. When he returned he would know whether he had been right or wrong. Or at least he would know the details of the crimes they were supposed to have committed. All he could remember was that in both cases a killing had been involved.

He walked slowly to the house, went in, and closed the door. He walked to the kitchen and reached for the lamp.

He saw the money as he did. Currency. Gold coins. He hadn't seen her leave it, but she was the only one who could have left it here.

He spread it on the table and counted it. There were $200 exactly.

He couldn't take it, of course, and would give it back to her. But the thought of her offering it made a pleasant tightness come to his throat.

He didn't deserve a girl like Sara. His record up to now had not been a particularly enviable one.

Ten years of drifting, of moving from job to job, of wildness, and quarrelsomeness because he was touchy about himself and the heritage he believed was his.

Twice he had drawn his gun in anger and twice had seen men die under it. Both times he had been released because the killing was in self-defense.

He'd run with the wild bunch, and, if he hadn't stopped a week ago, he'd have fulfilled the heritage he believed was his.

Now doubt was growing in his mind. Perhaps he had been wrong. Perhaps both his father and brother had been convicted on false evidence and were innocent of the crimes for which they had been hanged.

If such was the case, John Kennebeck had an ugly and monstrous debt to pay. Lew had to live long enough to collect that debt—and right now the chances of that didn't seem too good.

Kennebeck was the power in this country. He had money enough to buy false witnesses, to bribe lawmen and even judges to do what he ordered them to. He had power enough to force his will upon those who could not be bought. He was unscrupulous enough to use violence when other means failed.

And Lew was alone, burdened by a name that now, at least, was badly tarnished. People would be only too willing to believe the worst of him. Wasn't he a Moffit? Hadn't his father and brother ended their lives on the scaffold in Kennebeck?

He put the money in an empty lard can and set it on the shelf. He picked up the lamp and carried it upstairs. He stripped off boots and pants and shirt, then blew it out.

He lay down on the creaking bed and stared into the blackness of the room.

He slept almost immediately. Exhausted, he did not stir all through the night. Nor did he dream.

He awoke at sunup, groggy, aching, blurred of eye. He got up and went downstairs and out into the bright sunlight. He walked to the creek and splashed icy water over his head and onto his face.

He returned to the house, the events of yesterday returning to his mind. He thought with horror of the nearly successful hanging in Kennebeck yesterday, and a new, cold chill of fear ran through him. He thought of Sara, and of last night.

He built up the fire in the stove and made breakfast for himself. He ate it hastily.

A new sense of urgency was prodding him. There was not much time. Kennebeck wasn't going to sit and brood over his failure yesterday. He would strike again, and again. And if he should find out about Sara and Lew, he would throw what little caution was in him to the winds. He'd come and put a torch to this house and the buildings that surrounded it. He'd hunt Lew down and shoot him like he would a wolf.

The appalling enormity of the task he had set himself suddenly became overwhelming in Lew's mind. What chance did he, one man, have against Kennebeck and his crew? What chance did he have when everything he did would be colored in the eyes of the people of the country by the fact that he was a Moffit?

He thought of Sara again. He wouldn't give her up. Nor would he give up this place, or his chance to clear the Moffit name.

He finished his breakfast and washed the dishes. He went out, caught and saddled his horse, mounted, and rode west through the low hills that footed the plateau. Shortest way to Glen Cañon was west up a tributary of Hangman's Creek called No Name Creek. Thence from its headwaters over a low pass to the headwaters of Cañon Creek that led directly to the county seat. This way, it was a ride of about eighteen miles, and he rode into Glen Cañon in midmorning.

He went directly to the livery barn, where he ordered a good feed of hay and grain for his horse. Then, walking, he headed for the enormous old Victorian courthouse.

It stood in the center of a block-square plot of grass and trees and was four stories high. The upper story was festooned with balconies and gingerbread scrollwork. Above this towered a bell cupola around which a flock of pigeons flew.

In common with most courthouses, this one smelled of disinfectant used in the jail at the rear. Lew went to the door marked County Court immediately, entered the office, and waited at the counter until the man in charge came toward him.

He said: "I want to see some old records . . . the Moffit trials over at Kennebeck."

"How long ago was that?"

"Ten years on one. Eleven on the other."

The man left him and went into a record room that adjoined the office. He returned a few minutes later with a huge, dusty ledger. "Here's the first one. When you're finished with it, I'll get the other."

Lew thanked him. He carried the ledger to a desk, and sat down. He began to thumb through the pages.

A strange and mounting tension came to him. He began to turn the pages faster. What would he find? What would this ledger tell him?

He found it at last and began to read. Jess's crime had been rustling and murder. He had pleaded innocent.

Lew read on, wading through the mountain of detail and irrelevant testimony.

Evidence had been largely circumstantial, and Kennebeck's testimony had played an important part in it. Kennebeck claimed he had been losing cattle steadily and had suspected Jess Moffit who, he believed, was stealing them out of a twisted desire for revenge against Kennebeck who he blamed for his father's execution, though Kennebeck could not imagine why.

Watching Jess had yielded nothing in the way of proof. And then one day Kennebeck found the body of one of his crewmen on the Moffit place, and nearby a partially skinned-out steer.

In spite of the vagueness of the evidence, Jess had been arrested for the crime. He could offer no explanation, but swore he had neither butchered the steer nor killed the man who caught him at it.

Quite obviously, Jess would never have been convicted but for Kennebeck's testimony. Nor would he have been convicted if he had not publicly threatened Kennebeck. But since he was known as a bitter and vengeful man, it was natural enough for the jurymen to believe the worst of him. Besides, the dead man had been shot with a .44, the same caliber as the gun Jess carried.

Lew read the names of the jurymen. On a scrap of paper he copied them down. He only recognized a few of them.

He looked up from the ledger to find the clerk standing over him. "I'm closing the office for lunch. You'll have to come back at one o'clock."

Lew nodded and rose stiffly from the chair. So engrossed had he been that he hadn't thought of the time or realized how fast it passed. He went out and the clerk followed, locking the door behind them.

Lew circled the courthouse to the sheriff's office in the rear. He went inside.

The sheriff was tall and gaunt and, Lew judged, at least seventy years old. He didn't remember the man but that wasn't surprising. He hadn't been present at either Jess's or his father's trial.

He said: "I'm Lew Moffit, from over at Kennebeck."

"Will Locke." The sheriff stuck out a gaunt and bony hand.

"Were you sheriff ten years ago when they hanged my brother?"

"I sure was. Been sheriff twenty-two years." Locke stared at him steadily, with a strange kind of penetration. Lew felt a compulsion to drop his glance but resisted it and stubbornly held the sheriff's eyes.

He said: "They left me a ranch on Hangman's Creek. I've come back to it. First day in town John Kennebeck and his crew tried to hang me from that scaffold there. They'd have done it, too, if the marshal hadn't interfered."

An inquiring expression came into the sheriff's eyes.

Lew said: "I'm telling you because that's not the end of it. John Kennebeck hates my guts and he won't be satisfied with hate. He'll try to kill me or burn me out."

"The town of Kennebeck is a long way off, son, and I've only got one deputy."

"Your job's to protect the citizens of this county. If you can't do it, they've got a right to protect themselves. I intend to do it. If I were you, I'd ride over and tell John Kennebeck that. Tell him to stay off my land. Tell him to let me alone. Tell him he won't put a hand on me again. He'll be dead if he tries."

"You sound like your brother Jess."

"Do I, sheriff? Maybe that's a compliment. I came back here prepared to forget the past. But

150

Kennebeck doesn't intend to let me forget. So I'll oblige him. I'll remember. I've been remembering all morning while I read the transcript of Jess's trial. Pretty flimsy evidence to hang a man on, wouldn't you say, Sheriff? Not a witness that saw him kill that man. Not a track or anything that belonged to Jess to tie him in with it. How did you feel about that trial? Think Jess got a fair shake?"

Locke hesitated, then said reluctantly: "It's not my job to question the courts. I arrested Jess on a complaint sworn out by Kennebeck. I brought him to trial. Beyond that, I had nothing to do with it. I officiated at the hanging, but I didn't spring the trap."

"What if Kennebeck perjured himself?"

"Can you prove that he did?"

Lew shook his head. "But I might work on it."

"Bring me proof and I'll throw Kennebeck in jail. I don't give a damn how big he is."

"If he perjured himself at the trial, he must have killed that man himself."

"That's a pretty wild accusation. I wouldn't repeat it."

"I won't, Sheriff. Not until I can back it up." He stared at the sheriff for several moments. The compulsion to drop his glance was still with him but he didn't intend to yield to it. After several moments more the sheriff grinned faintly and looked away. Lew turned and went outside.

He had not expected protection. Obtaining it had not been his purpose in coming here. He had wanted to establish a basis for self-defense in anything that might arise in the days to come. Let Kennebeck be known as the aggressor.

He headed across the courthouse square toward a restaurant on the main street of the town, wondering what he would find this afternoon in the transcript of his father's trial.

VI

He returned to the courthouse at 1:00 and waited until the clerk unlocked the door and let him in. The man got him the second ledger, and he sat down at a desk with it.

Bank robbery and murder had been Morgan Moffit's crimes, but in this trial the evidence was less circumstantial at least.

Jim McGraw and another man had been working late at the bank. There had been a knock on the door and McGraw had answered it.

Light was poor in the foyer of the bank. But not too poor to see the revolver in the visitor's hand or the bandanna tied over the lower part of his face.

McGraw backed up, and the man came in.

McGraw turned to yell at the other man and was struck from behind and knocked to the floor, near to unconsciousness.

The other bank employee, a young man named Wilhite, snatched for a gun and was shot down and killed. While McGraw lay only partially conscious on the floor, the intruder cleaned out the safe and fled.

McGraw identified the bandit as Morgan Moffit, who owned a heavily mortgaged herd of cattle he was almost sure to lose.

A hastily formed posse rode up Hangman's Creek to the Moffit place. They found the sack of money hidden in the hay of the barn loft. Morgan Moffit was taken back to Kennebeck and lodged in the town jail to await his trial.

Pretty cut and dried. Except for Morgan Moffit's testimony. He swore he had been at home all evening. His son Jess corroborated his story. Lew, only fourteen, was asleep in bed and therefore didn't know.

Kennebeck's name was as notable for its absence in this trial as it had been for its prominence in the second. He had no evidence to give. He didn't even testify.

Scowling to himself, Lew returned the ledger and thanked the clerk. McGraw's identification of Morgan Moffit could have been wrong. He had admitted that the light was poor. He had admitted that the bandit was masked, that his hat was pulled very low over his eyes. He had not heard the man utter a single word.

He must, then, have identified Morgan Moffit through something other than the bandit's face—perhaps a hat, a jacket, or shirt—an impression rather than something concrete that he actually saw.

The money in the loft—someone could have planted it there. Lew caught himself thinking that Kennebeck had been close to his father's size and build. Kennebeck could have held up the bank, slugged McGraw, and killed Wilhite. He could have raced north up Hangman's Creek, slipped into the Moffit barn, and concealed the money there. He could even have been wearing some of Morgan Moffit's clothes.

But why? Why did Kennebeck hate Morgan Moffit? Why did his hate go on even after Moffit was dead, to encompass his sons, one after the other?

Puzzled and preoccupied, Lew walked to the livery stable and got his horse. He paid the hostler, mounted, and rode out of town, taking the road toward home.

He had discovered nothing today that would prove Kennebeck's responsibility for the two convictions. But he had satisfied himself at least that Kennebeck was responsible.

Perhaps it was wild and irresponsible to build such a case against Kennebeck in his mind.

Perhaps he believed Kennebeck had framed his father and brother only because he so wanted to believe their innocence. Yet he had seen Kennebeck in action yesterday. He had seen the lengths to which Kennebeck would go.

From here on, he would have to proceed carefully. If Kennebeck had successfully framed both his father and brother, it would be easy for him to frame Lew. And how, after eleven years, could Lew ever prove Kennebeck had done what Lew thought he had? Impossible, unless Kennebeck implicated himself—and he sure as hell wasn't going to do that.

He'd talk to McGraw next time he was in town, but he didn't expect that McGraw would change his story now. Eleven years had passed, and by this time McGraw was probably even more certain of his identification of Morgan Moffit than he had been before.

He shrugged inwardly. He would have enough difficulties without trying to disprove convictions ten and eleven years old. Kennebeck would see to that.

He arrived home an hour before sundown, prepared and ate his supper, and went immediately to bed.

After leaving Lew, Sara Kennebeck rode straight home, by a route she knew through fields and creek bottom that brought her into the huge ranch yard behind the haystacks and the barn. She put her horse into the corral and carried the saddle into the barn. Then she stood motionless and stared upcountry toward the Moffit place.

She felt bruised and hurt, and yet she felt something else, both fiercely possessive and softly sympathetic. She wanted to cry and was angry with herself because she did.

Exactly what she had expected of Lew she didn't know. She had wantonly thrown herself at him and she couldn't blame him for accepting what she offered him. She had known as he carried her toward the creek that there was more vengeful hatred in his heart than love. Yet she had let him carry her there and make love to her.

He said he had changed. He said he wanted to marry her. Did he mean that or was it only conflicting emotions of guilt, shame, and pity? She didn't know.

She was a fool for allowing her emotions to become involved with Lew, particularly right now. But it had begun many years ago, before he went away. She tossed her head impatiently. That had been puppy love, hero-worship maybe, the lure of the unknown. She was no longer a girl and her perspective should be that of a grown woman. She should have been able to see that Lew would either be dead or gone within a month. And what kind of prospect was that for a girl to stake her life and love upon?

The thought of his lying dead put an iciness into her chest. She could feel her breathing hasten and her heart speed up under the impetus of her fear. Perhaps she had been wrong in counseling him to stay. Perhaps if she had gone away with him . . . Her father wasn't God. They could successfully hide from him.

But she didn't believe it. What her father wanted, he got. What he sought to do, he did. He was omnipotent, and nothing could stand against him. Nothing ever had.

At least so far as she knew, nothing ever had. Yet, before she was born something must have happened between her father and Morgan Moffit to make such a violent hatred grow. She wondered what it had been.

What did men quarrel over, anyway? In the early days when settlers were just coming in, why did men quarrel? Over a piece of land? Possibly. Yet it was John Kennebeck who owned the best of the land on Hangman's Creek. And the best water rights, too. Morgan Moffit had possessed only a couple of sections up the creek.

Unlikely that land had caused their quarrel, or water, either. A woman then. But what woman? And why did her father hate Morgan Moffit so much more violently than Moffit had apparently hated him?

When you approached a problem logically, she decided, you came up with orderly and logical answers. John Kennebeck was the one with the unbearable hate. Therefore, Morgan Moffit must have gotten the woman they both wanted and had quarreled about—Lew's mother, who had died when he was born.

She turned and abruptly hurried toward the house. She passed the lighted bunkhouse, acknowledging the greetings of the cowpunchers sitting before it, smoking, on a bench. One got up, Lane Yost, and tried to walk with her, but she speeded her steps and reached the house before he could catch up. She went inside and closed the door.

The Chinese cook, Ling, was bustling around the kitchen. He glanced at her and gave her a toothy smile. She asked: "Is Father at home, Ling?"

"No, Missy. He go to town right after supper."

"How long has he been gone?" Thinking of what she meant to do, Sara felt sneaky and ashamed. She wondered if her expression showed it.

"Half hour, Missy. Jus' left."

"Thank you." She continued on through the enormous kitchen into the equally enormous living room. Where should she start? In her father's office or in his bedroom?

She decided on the office and headed immediately toward it. She walked down a long, wide hall that was carpeted with Navajo rugs and the hides of animals, until she came to the office door. She opened it, struck a match, and lighted the lamp.

Feeling guilty—almost like a thief—she began to go through the cubbyholes and drawers of the desk. The minutes passed, dragged into half an hour and beyond.

On the bottom of the lower right-hand drawer she found it, the thing she had been looking for. Framed exquisitely in gold, it was the picture of a woman, a beautiful woman. Sara could tell that in spite of the formal pose and severe expression that was on her face.

This must be it, she thought. This must be the woman over whom her father and Morgan Moffit had fought. This must be Lew's mother.

With this unexpected knowledge in her hands, she began to remember other things. Her own mother. The strain that had always seemed to be between her parents. The hurt and the bitterness that had sometimes slipped out in her mother's actions or conversation.

You're imagining this, she told herself. *You're building something out of imagination and wishful thinking.* But she knew that was not strictly true. She could not recall one single moment of affection between her father and mother. And she remembered sharply and suddenly an overheard remark at her mother's funeral in the town's one church: "Poor soul, she just never had anything to live for." A cryptic remark to Sara, who didn't understand the things adults did anyway. But if now she was right, the remark pretty much explained itself. Her mother had finally realized she was fighting a battle she couldn't win. She had just given up.

She stared closely at the picture in her hand. What kind of woman was she, who could command that kind of undying love? Puzzled, and confused, she shook her head.

She returned the picture to the drawer, blew out the lamp, and left the room, puzzling as to how her father had gotten the picture. Was it one Lew's mother had given him long ago before she married Morgan Moffit? Or had it belonged to Morgan Moffit before he was hanged?

Returning along the hall, she met her father who had just come in. He frowned at her. "Where have you been?"

"Just now?" She realized suddenly that she was afraid of him, that she had always been afraid of him. But she met his glance steadily enough and said: "In your office."

"I mean before that."

She would not have lied to him if he had asked her why she was in his office, for that involved only herself. But she knew she did not dare tell him she had been with Lew for that involved added danger to Lew. She said: "Just riding. No place in particular."

"Where?"

"Up under the rim. I like to watch the sunset from there. Why do you ask?"

He evaded her glance. "No particular reason. Only I wish to God you'd quit gallivantin' all over the countryside. It ain't lady-like in the first place. And it ain't safe."

"I've always been safe before."

"You wasn't growed up before."

She started to pass him but he caught her arm. "What were you doing in my office?"

She began to tremble and hoped he wouldn't notice. She said: "I was going through your desk."

"What for?"

"Looking for the reason you hate the Moffit family so."

His hand tightened on her arm, almost making her cry out. His voice was soft, but very dangerous. "Find it?"

"I think so. In the bottom drawer. A picture of a woman. Was she Morgan Moffit's wife? Was she Lew's mother? You could have hated Morgan because she married him instead of you. You could hate Lew because she died bearing him. But why did you hate Jess?"

She staggered against the wall as her father flung her violently away. She straightened in time to receive a full-armed slap on the side of her face that knocked her sprawling to the floor.

161

Stunned, she lay there, staring up at him. He stepped over her and went on along the hall. The door of his office slammed thunderously with an impact that shook the house.

She lay still for a moment, unable to move. Tears blurred her eyes, choked her throat. Her body trembled violently.

She had been a fool—for searching his desk—for being so honest about it when she was caught.

She got painfully to her feet. Her head was ringing from the slap. The side of her face burned.

Always afraid of her father, she was now doubly so, for she understood fully the unleashed violence that lived in him.

Thirty years had passed since Lew's mother had made her choice and married Morgan Moffit. So far as John Kennebeck was concerned it might have happened yesterday. Brooding had kept alive his hatred and it was as strong now as it had ever been, perhaps even stronger.

He was capable of anything, she realized with a shock. Capable of committing the crime for which Morgan Moffit had been hanged and deliberately throwing the blame on Moffit. Capable of engineering the conviction of Jess Moffit.

Fear for Lew touched her heart with its icy hand. If he was capable of disposing of Morgan and Jess, he was capable of getting rid of Lew in the same way, or in any other way. Lew couldn't fight him. Nobody could—because sane people are hampered by restraints that law and decency impose on human beings almost from the day they are born. John Kennebeck was hampered by nothing. Not where the Moffits were concerned. While he might not be insane in the strictest sense of the word, he was certainly insane when it came to anything that bore the Moffit name.

She climbed the stairs to her room and absently lighted the lamp. She considered going to Lew and warning him again.

She decided against it reluctantly. She couldn't tell him anything that he did not already know.

If he stayed, though, he was doomed. She was very sure of that. Lew was tough and competent and as fearless as a man could be. But he couldn't stand alone against what John Kennebeck could and would throw against him.

She stared emptily at the wall, haunting fear narrowing and pinching her lovely eyes. What could she do? What could they do?

Run away together. It was the only answer. Somewhere in this land of a million square miles there must be one safe place where they could hide.

She closed her eyes. She could see in her mind the way her father's face had looked when she mentioned Morgan Moffit's wife.

Wild. Unrestrained. He had forgotten that she was his daughter or that she was a woman. He had forgotten everything but his raw, ungovernable fury.

He was probably down there now, staring at the picture she had found in the bottom drawer of his desk. What was he thinking, she wondered, as he looked at it? Had his face softened with love for a woman dead nearly twenty-five years? Or were his eyes hard with hatred for the man who had married her, for the man whose birth had stolen the life from her? Was his face filled with anger and even hatred for the woman herself because she had not chosen him?

Sara thought that if she knew that, she might know a great deal more about her father than she did right now. But she would never know. John Kennebeck had kept his secret all these years. He would keep it until he died.

VII

John Kennebeck stood for several moments just inside the office door, the thunderous sound of its slamming still ringing in his ears. His head felt light and his skin burned. He could feel his hands and arms trembling. He wanted to smash something; he wanted to wreck this room the way an enraged bull might have wrecked it if it were penned up inside.

He controlled himself with an effort, crossed the room, struck a match, and lit the lamp on the desk. The compulsion to pick up the lamp and fling it against the wall was almost overpowering, but he resisted it.

He paced to the window and glowered into the blackness outside. The trembling in his hands and arms did not diminish. His eyes remained hard and bright with fury.

He returned to his desk and forced himself to sit down. He gripped the arms of the chair until his knuckles turned white.

Suddenly he bent, slammed open the bottom drawer, and withdrew the picture Sara had found earlier. He stared at it, his face gradually losing its flush, his eyes losing their hardness and their rage. His hands stopped trembling.

Why had life dealt with him so cruelly, he wondered suddenly. He had built this ranch into something both big and successful, but it wasn't what he wanted. He had never really cared for the money or power it brought him. All he had wanted was Jenny, and she had chosen Morgan Moffit instead of him.

Why? What had Morgan offered her that he had not? Jenny was dead and Morgan was, too, but whenever he thought of them together in the soft darkness of the night he felt his rage rising as though they both were still alive, as though Jenny had refused him and married Morgan only yesterday.

He puzzled briefly over that. What was it about him that made it so impossible for him to forget? Why had the years not softened the pain as they did with other men?

Frowning, he thought of Lew. Lew was the reason he could not forget, he reasoned. As long as Lew was alive, the torment would stay alive in his mind. Only when Lew was dead would he be able to forget. With Lew gone there would be nothing of Jenny, nothing of Morgan Moffit left to torment him. Perhaps then he could know a little peace.

He stared at the picture a moment more, then replaced it in the drawer. He leaned back in his chair and lighted a cigar. His eyes narrowed thoughtfully.

Characteristically he gave little thought to Sara, or to the fact that he had knocked her to the floor. She had angered him and he had struck her down. It was as simple as that and it caused him no concern.

Yet, in his way, he loved Sara and was usually good to her. He still thought of her as a child, and only when she stepped out of this rôle did conflict arise between them.

She had stepped out of it when Lew Moffit came home. She had asserted her right to become an adult and to make adult decisions for herself. That was something else Lew Moffit had to answer for.

Moffit had to go. Tomorrow if possible. There wasn't time for planning and plotting so that the law would take care of him. There had to be a more direct and quicker way.

Kennebeck scowled as his mind touched upon each member of his crew, settling at last upon Lane Yost. Lane was the man for this job, he thought. Lane fancied himself quite a gunfighter and was jealous of Sara, anyway. He wouldn't have to be sent after Lew. Kennebeck would only have to stir up a little jealousy in him—tell him Sara was seeing Lew Moffit every day. Yost would take it from there.

He tossed his cigar into the brass spittoon, blew out the lamp, and left the office. He walked slowly up the stairs to his room. He removed his clothes and went to bed.

His mind was more at ease than it had been since Lew Moffit's return. Perhaps Yost wasn't man enough to kill Lew, but then again perhaps he was. However it turned out, it would serve his purposes. If Lew was killed, all well and good. If Lew killed Yost, then he would swear out a warrant charging Lew with the murder of Yost. A conviction would be a virtual certainty in view of the community's opinion of the Moffits, and then he would have the pleasure of seeing

Lew dangling at the end of the hangman's rope.

He closed his eyes and almost immediately went to sleep.

Lew awoke early, and for a few moments lay still, with his eyes open, staring at the ceiling. The events of yesterday came back to him and with them came a strange feeling of uneasiness that almost amounted to a premonition.

It was easy enough to understand the source of his uneasiness. It sprang from his knowledge of Kennebeck, from his comprehension of the extent of Kennebeck's hatred for the Moffit clan. He had unearthed no proof yesterday, proof that would stand up in court, but the signs had been plain enough for Lew. Kennebeck was behind his father's conviction. He was behind Jess's conviction as well. He had cold-bloodedly murdered both Lew's father and brother, using the law itself for the murder weapon. And as though that were not enough, he had killed two innocent men, the bank clerk, Wilhite, and his own crewman in accomplishing it.

There would be no place where Kennebeck would draw the line in getting rid of Lew. Anything would go, from outright bushwhacking on up.

Lew got up and began to dress, his uneasiness changing to a feeling of futility, futility that was foreign to him. He kicked out angrily at a chair but pulled the kick before it struck. Jess had never given up even though he must have known, as Lew did, how determined was Kennebeck's vengefulness. He hadn't run away and Lew wasn't going to, either.

He buckled on his gun belt and went downstairs. He shaved a stick of wood into the kitchen range and lighted the shavings. He piled more wood on and closed the stove, then picked up the water bucket and went outside.

He headed for the creek. Halfway there he stopped, listening, his head cocked like a hound's as he waited for the sound that had halted him to repeat itself. It did not and he went on.

The creek made a low roar as it tumbled along, one he usually found pleasant but that today made him uneasy because it obscured most other sounds. He filled the bucket and put it down. Kneeling, he splashed cold water onto his face. He lathered quickly with a bar of soap he had left on a nearby rock, rinsed and toweled himself dry with the flour sack slung over his shoulder.

He took time to have a look around, then picked up the bucket in his left hand, and headed for the house, his uneasiness steadily increasing as he walked.

He reached the house without incident, went in, and closed the door. He put the bucket down, then went to the window and stared outside, taking care to remain mostly hidden behind the window jamb. He saw nothing move, saw nothing that had not been there last night. He thought irritably: *You damned old woman, you're making this up out of nothing at all!*

But he knew it wasn't true. He had heard something just after he had left the house. He didn't know what it was but he did know the sound was foreign to the place or his ear would not have sorted it out from other, normal sounds.

He stayed at the window for a long, long time. Then he crossed the room and put on the coffee pot. He made himself a smoke and returned to the window, puffing on it. The coffee pot began to simmer and sing on the hot stove top.

He waited thoughtfully for the coffee to boil. When it did, he poured himself a cup and sipped the steaming stuff. He knew he ought to cook breakfast, but he didn't feel like eating now.

He heard the beat of a horse's hoofs and went to the window again. Sara Kennebeck was riding into the yard.

Lew's feeling of uneasiness had not diminished and, reasoning, he decided there was basis for it. Probably the house was being watched. Going out for water, he had, no doubt, heard some sound the watcher inadvertently made.

He opened the door, his expression far from a welcoming one. He asked coldly: "What are you doing here?"

Her eyes showed instant hurt, and a slight flush stained her face. She said haltingly: "I wanted to see you, Lew. I had to see you. I think I know . . ."

He said: "Some other time. Right now you get on home."

"Why? Lew, what's the matter?"

"Nothing's the matter. I just don't want you here today."

She stared at him for a moment, disbelievingly. Then, her eyes growing angry, she said: "All right. I'll go. But . . ." She waited for several moments, obviously for Lew to relent but he did not. The flush was very dark in her face as she turned her horse, rode toward the creek, and disappeared.

Lew touched the grip of his gun and stepped away from the door. He was certain now that someone was out there in the brush watching him. He didn't know how the attack would come, but he knew it would. Only he wasn't going to hide in the house all day. He'd stay out here where whoever it was could see him. He doubted if Kennebeck would have him dry-gulched—not at this stage of the game. Kennebeck would want more satisfaction out of it than that.

Sara had been gone less than five minutes when Lew heard a sharp crack out in the brush at the far edge of the yard. He swung around, his hand nearly touching the grip of his gun.

A stranger was coming toward him, walking. The man's horse was nowhere in sight and Lew supposed it was tied farther back in the brush.

The stranger was half a head shorter than Lew, whip-slender and young. He walked with a certain arrogance that just missed being a swagger and he wore a mocking smile on his smooth-shaven face. Yet the eyes above that smile were at once angry, reckless, and unpredictable.

When he was twenty-five feet away, he said: "So you're Lew Moffit. You don't look so god-damned tough to me."

"And who are you?" Lew understood the play immediately. This man worked for Kennebeck and Kennebeck had sent him here to pick a quarrel.

"Lane Yost. Maybe you've heard of me."

"Why should I?" Lew scowled impatiently. "Let's just pass all the steps that lead up to what you've got in mind and get on with it. I've got things to do."

Yost's eyes flickered and the smile faded. He said: "You've been after Sara and by God I won't stand for that!"

"You won't have a choice. Because if you don't turn around and get out of here, you'll be too dead to object to anything." As Lew spoke, he glanced beyond Yost toward the brush, searching for others who might be waiting to make sure

Yost made his kill. He saw nothing but knew that didn't mean no one was there.

Yost growled: "You son-of-a-bitch!"

Lew was suddenly weary of all this. He said harshly: "Don't stand there jawing about it all day. If you're going to use your gun, use it."

Yost flung himself violently to one side, letting himself fall as he did, but yanking his gun before he hit the ground. He rolled and at the end of his roll the gun was extended before him and dropping into line.

Lew hesitated only a fraction of a second as Yost began to move. Then, realizing that this was Yost's play, he yanked his gun, thumbed back the hammer, and fired instantly.

His bullet raked a long furrow in the ground six inches from Yost's extended body. Lew was looking straight into the muzzle of Yost's extended gun.

Lew fired a second time, but was moving as he did, lunging to one side, trying to escape the certainty of death promised by the gaping muzzle of Yost's gun.

It roared, pushing a cloud of powder smoke in front of it, and the bullet ticked the muscles of Lew's upper arm, stinging like a bee.

The pain was not great, but it had the effect of releasing all the restraint that was left in him. He was instantly and furiously angry.

He halted all movement and, spread-legged

and solid, fired deliberately as Yost swung his gun for a second shot.

The bullet struck Yost squarely in the throat and, because of Yost's prone position and the angle at which Lew had fired, did not emerge at the back of his neck but coursed down into his body.

Blood gushed briefly from the man's throat. Then his head fell into the dust, concealing the spreading pool.

Now, if anything, Lew's rage increased. He had never seen Yost before in his life and certainly had no reason to want him dead. This was another death to be chalked up to Kennebeck, and the thought that Kennebeck had used him for the murder weapon made him furious.

Behind him he heard hoof beats and swung warily around. But the rider was Sara, returning, her face a ghastly shade of gray, her eyes enormous with fear.

She flung herself from the horse, stumbled, and fell. Lew holstered his gun, went over and helped her to her feet. Blood was already soaking the upper sleeve of his shirt.

Her hand touched it and came away and she stared at the hand in horror. Her eyes lifted to his face. "Lew! You're hurt! Is it bad?"

"No. It isn't bad."

"You come on in the house and let me look at it."

He grinned, the anger, the tension draining out of him. He let her lead him toward the house and suddenly having someone care what happened to him was a very pleasant thing.

VIII

Sara helped him out of his shirt, washed and bandaged the wound, which was only a shallow furrow less than two inches long. Finished, she asked: "Can you eat? I'll fix breakfast if you can."

He said—"I'm starved."—watching her steadily.

She built up the fire and began to prepare breakfast. As she worked, she said: "Lane Yost worked for Father and Father will probably try to have you convicted for murdering him. But he won't get away with it. I saw the whole thing. I got to thinking as I rode away that you were acting strange. I turned around and started back to find out why. I saw the whole thing and I'll tell the sheriff how it really was."

Lew studied her face. He might have been willing to go to trial to save Sara from her father's wrath, but her expression told him it would be useless even to suggest such a thing. She'd never stand for it.

She put a fresh cup of coffee and a stack of

buckwheat cakes in front of him. He discovered that he was hungry and began to eat. Yet a little core of anger remained in the back of his thoughts.

Kennebeck wasn't giving up. Sara's statement might keep Lew from going to jail for killing Yost, but it wouldn't stop Kennebeck. He'd try something else and he'd keep on trying until he was dead or until Lew was.

While he ate, Sara busied herself tidying up the messy kitchen. When she had finished, he said: "Go home now. I've got things to do. And don't say anything about being here or about seeing what happened unless there's need for it. Right now there isn't."

"All right, Lew." She went reluctantly to the door and he followed her. Turning, she said worriedly: "You'll be all right?"

He nodded.

"Be careful."

"Sure." He gripped her shoulders and kissed her on the mouth. "Now go on."

He watched her mount and ride out. She took the direction of the creek so that she could ride home unobserved.

As soon as she was out of sight, Lew hurried to the corral and saddled his horse. Mounting, he rode into the brush in the direction from which Yost had come. He had gone no more than a couple of hundred yards before he found

Yost's horse tied to a clump of brush. Towing the animal behind him, he returned to Yost's body.

The horses shied from the smell of blood and pranced nervously. After several unsuccessful tries, Lew got Yost's body slung across the saddle of his horse and tied it down.

Leading Yost's animal, he rode up to the road. He spurred and ran both horses steadily for several miles. At last, judging he was well ahead of Sara, he swung right and took to the brush and willow fringed creek bottom where he could ride without being seen. This way, he crossed Kennebeck's ranch boundary and continued until he was just below the house.

What he intended doing was dangerous; he was well aware of that. But he wanted Kennebeck to know, at this point and all along the line, that he wasn't bluffed, that he wasn't afraid.

A wagon road led from the creek to the house. He halted a moment, glanced back to see that the body was still secure, then spurred his horse and thundered along the climbing road toward the house and ranch buildings at its end.

He saw nothing until he was well into the yard. Then he saw Kennebeck, standing in front of the bunkhouse talking to several members of his crew. Kennebeck swung around at the sound of the horses' galloping hoofs and instantly snatched for the gun hanging at his side. He bellowed: "Get him! Get the son-of-a-bitch!"

Lew released the reins of the horse he was leading, and reined his own horse sharply to one side. Behind him, Kennebeck's gun roared repeatedly as the man emptied it frantically at him. Lew swung around in his saddle and waved mockingly. Then he was through the yard and thundering along the lane that led through the hay fields to the road.

He glanced back when he reached the road. He could see men running like ants back and forth across the yard. He could hear Kennebeck bellowing like a bull. A rifle began to crack and bullets kicked up dust a dozen feet behind Lew's running horse.

He couldn't help grinning despite the fact that he knew they'd pursue him ruthlessly. Perhaps he hadn't been wise in thus prodding Kennebeck's wrath. But neither was it wise to stay on the defensive all the time.

He galloped up the road until the jutting point of a ridge hid him from Kennebeck's ranch yard. Then he swung sharply to the right and began to climb. Under the sharp and persistent prodding of his spurs, the horse leaped up the slope in great lunges. A few moments later Lew was surrounded by the twisted cedars and piñon pine that grew thickly on these benches at the foot of the high plateau.

He slowed the horse to a steady walk and began, skillfully, to hide his trail. In spots he rode over bare shale rock where his horse would leave no tracks. When the bare shale petered out, he clung to land beneath the cedars and piñons, land heavily carpeted with needles and decaying leaves. Sometimes he rode straight through nearly impenetrable oak brush pockets, and occasionally reversed directions inside the pockets, coming back out on an opposite heading from that on which he had entered them.

They were coming now and he could hear the angry shouts of the men, sometimes the sharp crack of a branch or the clang of metal against metal.

Immediately he gave up hiding his trail and rode a straight course toward a trail he knew that led out on top of the plateau. He didn't suppose he could return home tonight because, when they gave up the search, that was where they'd look for him. He'd probably have to spend the night out in the brush and return home in the early hours of the dawn. Kennebeck's fury would have tempered by then, and he might be thinking straight. If it hadn't, then perhaps tomorrow was as good a time for a showdown with him as any other time would be.

High brush screened the trail to the plateau top and Lew was above the rim before he glimpsed the searchers far below. They were still patiently trying to unravel his twisted trail and it was slow going for them. He watched for several moments, then continued out on top.

Here the land was rolling, covered with scrubby brush in contrast to the high brush of the valley floor. There were pockets of aspen and spruce on north-facing slopes, and there were Kennebeck cattle everywhere.

But for Kennebeck, many of the cattle up here might have been Moffit cattle, he thought. He wondered what had become of those that were left after Jess's death. Kennebeck had probably found some way of getting his hands on them, legally or otherwise.

He made good time, still taking reasonable care to hide his trail, staying off the bare ridge tops and traveling directly through the brush and timber pockets that lay ahead of him. At last he rode out on a narrow point from which he could look straight down into his own ranch yard. From here, he could see what was going on with no danger of detection from below.

He unsaddled his horse and picketed him to graze. Taking his rifle, he walked to the edge of the rim and settled himself comfortably.

At times he dozed, but it was always lightly, and no small sound escaped his ears. The afternoon wore away and the sun sank steadily toward the western horizon.

They gave up sooner than he had anticipated, and at sundown he saw a cloud of dust rising half a dozen miles downcountry from his house on the valley floor. He counted them as they came nearer, and counted eight.

He smiled ruefully at that. Eight men to kill one. He had, at least, instilled some respect in Kennebeck.

They reached his gate and rode on through. They pulled up in the ranch yard, dismounted, and scurried like ants from building to building as they searched. After about twenty minutes, they remounted and rode out. Seven rode out the way they had come in. The eighth rode across the creek and climbed through the benches toward the rim. Lew watched him for a long, long time, climbing up across the benches. At last he saw him drop from sight into the valley of No Name Creek, and knew he was headed for Glen Cañon, probably to lodge a murder complaint against Lew with the sheriff there.

Lew got up stiffly, walked to his horse, and coiled the picket rope. He led the animal to where he'd left his saddle and flung it up. He mounted and returned to the trail by which he had ascended the plateau. There would be no further threat from Kennebeck tonight. He was going to try using the law this time. For tonight, at least, Lew was safe, and so went home.

He slept deeply that night, but awoke with the dawn, washed, and got breakfast for himself. He had scarcely finished it when he heard a horse entering the yard. He went out and saw

Will Locke, the sheriff from Glen Cañon, riding in.

Locke's gaunt face was even gaunter this morning and his eyes were tired. He dismounted stiffly, grunting sourly: "I'm gettin' too damned old for these all-night rides."

"Want some coffee?"

The sheriff nodded, those penetrating, searching eyes resting steadily on Lew.

He followed Lew into the house and sat down. He drank half a cup of coffee before he said: "You didn't waste any time, did you?"

"Kennebeck didn't waste any. He sent Yost up here. Yost came walking out of the brush calling me names and talking up a fight."

"Any proof of that?"

"What kind of proof do you need, for God's sake? I've got a bullet crease on my arm, and, if you'll look at Yost, you'll see he got it from the front."

The sheriff shrugged. "Might have been enough if you'd left the body lay and come after me. Way it is, I guess I'll have to hold you for trial. On Kennebeck's complaint."

"And by the time he gets through buying witnesses, Yost will have been unarmed."

The sheriff didn't reply. Lew said reluctantly: "Talk to Sara Kennebeck. She was here and she saw it all."

The sheriff's eyebrows raised briefly.

Lew said: "She wasn't here all night if that's what's on your mind."

"Didn't say she was."

"But you were thinking it."

"Mebbe. Is that what's bothering Kennebeck?"

"No, it isn't. I doubt if he even knows I've been seeing her."

Locke said: "All right. I'll talk to her." He studied Lew's face briefly. "You'll stay here until I get back?"

"I'll stay."

Locke went out and swung stiffly to his horse. He raised a hand in a curt gesture of farewell and rode up the lane toward the road.

Lew stood in the sun-washed yard and watched until he was out of sight. He hadn't wanted to let Sara become involved, but he hadn't had much choice. If he went to jail, he was beaten. Kennebeck would get him convicted as easily as he'd gotten Morgan Moffit and Jess convicted. His influence in the country was strong and he was unscrupulous enough to do anything.

Lew walked across the yard to the barn. He found some rusty tools and some nails and began to repair the barn doors. He wanted to go to town after wire and staples so that he could begin repairing the fence, but he had promised the sheriff he would stay. The trip to town would have to wait.

IX

Sara Kennebeck reached home at the height of the confusion created by Lew's sudden arrival with the body of Lane Yost. She put her horse into the corral and from there watched her enraged father lead his men in pursuit.

More frightened than ever before in her life, she waited, occasionally hearing a shout dimly echoed back from the high rims. Her breathing was shallow and her hands shook as she continued to wait—for the burst of shots that would signify they had caught up with Lew and were killing him.

A week ago, she thought, Lew Moffit had only been a memory in her mind, but he had become so much more than that. If they killed him now . . .

Suddenly she felt almost hysterical with her helplessness. There ought to be something she could do to help. There ought to be something!

But there wasn't. She knew that with an overpowering feeling of despair. She knew her father too well to believe he could change or even soften in his feelings toward the Moffits even though most of them were dead. He would go on like this until he killed Lew—or until Lew killed him.

It was unnatural, almost insane, the way he still hated over a woman he had loved and lost so many years ago. Couldn't he see that in Lew a part of her still lived? Couldn't he understand that by killing Lew he killed the last remaining reality of her on earth?

She shook her head helplessly. It was already early afternoon. They had been hunting up there for several hours and they hadn't come up with him yet. He must have weaved a twisted trail to have the unraveling of it take this long. Yet she knew her father's determination and she knew his ruthlessness.

Something high on the trail leading through the rims caught her eye and she stared closely, trying to make it out. Brush hid most of the trail, but finally she saw a rider emerge from it into a clear spot on the trail. It looked like Lew, but at this distance she could not be sure.

She continued to watch, waiting for others to follow him along that trail. But she saw nothing further and did not see Lew again. Then, with a suddenness that left her weak, a faint shout came down to her from the benches below the rim and she knew that Lew had gotten away. He was clear, and safe. It *was* Lew she had seen riding up the rimrock trail, and her father's men were still hunting him far below.

She went to the house and began doing all the things she should have done earlier in the day.

Occasionally she would return to the yard and stand listening until she had satisfied herself that her father and his men were still in the benches below the rim.

When they failed to find him . . . what then? she wondered. Would her father's fury extend to burning his ranch buildings with the intention of driving him away for good? She supposed it might, and in a way she hoped it would. Perhaps then Lew would consider taking her and leaving the country. Perhaps then he would be willing to risk having John Kennebeck after the two of them. Sara now believed, even if Lew did not, that they could elude him. Her father wasn't God and today had proved that he couldn't do everything he tried to do.

Later in the afternoon, she saw her father lead his men out of the benches and up the road toward Lew's ranch. Now, perhaps, he would burn Lew out. Or maybe he was only going there, thinking that was where Lew had gone.

She watched the northern sky after it got dark, but she saw no glow in it that would tell her Lew's buildings were afire. And later she heard her father and his men return.

She avoided him by going to her room and staying there. He must have gone to bed early himself, because by 9:00 the house was dark.

She slept very little that night and was awake

when the first gray streaked the eastern sky. She got up and went downstairs. Ling already had a cheerful fire going in the kitchen stove, and a pot of boiling coffee made the air fragrant with its smell. Sara went to the stove and poured herself a cup. She went out and sat on the back stoop while she sipped it and watched dawn turn the sky from gray to blue.

Ling came out to stand beside her. He said: "Missy, you know your father send after sheriff yesterday?"

She glanced up in surprise. "No, I didn't."

"Yes. He swear out warrant against Moffit for killing Yost."

She smiled faintly to herself, but she couldn't help the coldness that began growing in her chest. She could thwart her father's plan to have Lew thrown in jail by telling the sheriff that she had seen the fight. Yet, doing so, she would put Lew in even greater jeopardy, for then her father would have further cause to hate. He would know that she had been seeing Lew. He might even suspect that she intended to marry him, or that Lew and she . . .

Her face flushed with the memory of that night. Yet there was no regret in her. She would do exactly the same thing again.

She got up, went inside, and helped Ling get breakfast. She sat with her father in the dining room and ate. Neither talked much and neither mentioned Lew Moffit or anything that had happened yesterday.

Nervousness increased steadily in her. Her father finished eating and went outside. She stationed herself at the front window where she could see the road.

After what seemed an interminable wait, she saw a rider coming down the road, and not long afterward was able to recognize him as Sheriff Locke from the county seat at Glen Cañon. Locke turned in at the gate and rode unhurriedly toward the house.

Sara's stomach felt like ice. She went outside and stood on the porch, waiting for Locke. Glancing across the yard, she saw her father approaching from the barn.

Locke drew to a halt in front of her and touched the brim of his hat respectfully. " 'Mornin', Miss Kennebeck."

"Good morning, Mister Locke."

"I've been talking to Lew Moffit. He says you saw the fight between him and Lane Yost."

She nodded just as her father arrived, glowering. He said harshly: "Locke, I lodged a murder complaint against Moffit. Why haven't you taken him into custody?"

Locke glanced at him and back at Sara. "Exactly what happened, Miss Kennebeck?"

Kennebeck strode between Locke's horse and Sara. Facing the sheriff, he stood like a rock, legs spread, a savage scowl on his face. He roared: "Damn you! Answer me when I speak to you! What the hell are you asking her for? She don't know anything!"

Locke's face reddened slightly and his eyes narrowed. But his voice was calm when he replied. "She saw the fight between Moffit and Yost."

Kennebeck swung around. His face was almost purple. "Saw it? How could you see it? At that time of morning . . ."

Sara said: "I rode up there to tell him about the picture in the bottom drawer of your desk." She waited breathlessly for him to strike her, and watched the savage way he fought himself for control.

At last Kennebeck turned his back to her and faced Locke again. "She doesn't have to say a thing!"

Sara said: "But I want to. Yost started the quarrel and Yost made the first move toward his gun. All Lew Moffit did was defend himself." The words came out in a breathless rush.

Locke stared at Kennebeck. "That's pretty cut and dried. I'm not going to arrest Moffit for defending his life in his own back yard. And I advise you to be careful what you do, Mister Kennebeck. Let Moffit alone or I'll be coming after you."

He glanced over Kennebeck's head at Sara.

"Thanks, Miss Kennebeck. I'm glad you happened to be there." He touched the brim of his hat again, turned his horse, and rode away. He lifted the horse to a trot and, when he reached the road, turned upcountry in the direction from which he had come.

Kennebeck turned and glowered at Sara. She forced her eyes to meet his and tried to keep defiance out of them, probably failing, because he said between his teeth: "You bitch!"

She could feel the blood draining from her face. She started to speak but he interrupted her. "You spent the night with him, didn't you?"

"No, I didn't! I got up early and rode up there."

"But you have been with him. Don't lie to me. The pair of you have gotten too damned thick for no more time than he's been home."

"No." She tried to make her denial sound emphatic, not because she was ashamed of anything she had done or because she wished to escape whatever consequences there might be, but only because her father hated Lew enough already without anything making it worse.

He took two swift strides and swung the flat of his hand against her cheek. It rocked her head violently to one side and left the whole side of her face numb. He spoke savagely between his teeth. "You're a liar and a slut! You've been bedding with him out in the brush like any damned stray dog!"

Her face flamed with anger and her eyes sparkled. She said furiously: "That's a lie, Father! But I'll tell you this much! I'm going to marry him. I'm going to marry him and nothing you can do will stop me. And I'll go on seeing him. I'm not a little girl any more. I'm a woman and I have a right to make my own decisions!"

"Not while I'm alive!" He unbuckled his belt with trembling hands and yanked it clear of the loops. He swung it savagely, not apparently caring where it struck. His face was almost purple with rage.

The flat of it struck her side, wrapping itself around her waist. She turned and tried to run but he caught her blouse with his left hand and swung again with his right.

The blouse tore and she went to her knees. Kennebeck laid the belt across her back half a dozen times while she tried to reach the door. She caught one frightening glimpse of his face as she pulled herself up by grasping the door-knob. He was sweating heavily and his eyes held neither sanity nor restraint. She was suddenly more afraid of him than she had ever been in her life.

He choked: "Get up to your room! Damn you, get up to your room! I'll fix you so you'll never see him again!"

She got the door open and ran in utter terror for

the stairs. She stumbled up them ten feet ahead of him, ran into her room, and slammed the door. She stood with her back to it, breathing harshly and raggedly and trembling with hysteria.

She heard him come to the door, heard his breathing for several moments, then heard his footsteps go away as he descended the stairs.

She crossed the room and flung herself face down upon the bed, sobbing bitterly. She had let him bait her into admitting that she loved Lew and wanted to marry him. She had admitted that she had been seeing Lew. Instead of protecting him as she had meant to do, she had let her anger run away with her.

Her body burned where the belt had struck. She heard her father roaring in the yard: "Raney! Come here!"

After several moments she heard him shout: "Get on upstairs and stay in front of Sara's door! Don't let her out, no matter what anyone tells you. Understand? You stay there until night, and then I'll have somebody take your place."

The front door opened and slammed and she heard Raney's footsteps ascending the stairs. She was a prisoner. Jim Raney and all the rest of her father's crewmen, for that matter, were too afraid of him ever to disobey. Especially when he was like this.

She wondered what her father was going to do

now. He might cool down enough to remember the sheriff's warning, and then again he might not. She could only pray that he would, or that, if he didn't, Lew would remain on guard.

X

For a long time after Raney entered the house, John Kennebeck stood, trembling with fury, in the yard. The urge to destroy something—anything—was an overpowering compulsion in his mind. He thought what it would be like to have Lew Moffit within reach right now and experienced a brief and vicious joy. He'd show the son-of-a-bitch. He'd get to him one way or another or know the reason why.

Except for Sara, he would have had him today. If Locke had taken Lew to jail—it would have been cut and dried just as it had been with Lew's brother Jess. He could have bought plenty of men who would have sworn Yost had no gun when he left the ranch, that his body had no gun on it when Lew brought it back. That would have been enough. Lew would have been convicted of murder and hanged. On the scaffold Kennebeck had been saving for him all these years.

He frowned suddenly. More than once the citizens of Kennebeck had wanted to tear it down, but Kennebeck's influence was great enough that he'd been able to stop that kind of talk every time it got a start. Still, you couldn't be sure. . . . He remembered the look that had been on Will Locke's face just before he left. It was a look Kennebeck wasn't used to seeing in other people's faces. Disapproval. Even dislike. It was pretty plain that Locke was on Lew Moffit's side. And against Kennebeck.

Locke had better be careful, he thought. If he wanted to, he could prevent Locke from getting in as sheriff again. He had enough power and influence to make sure of that.

He tramped angrily across the yard, a disturbing thought troubling his mind. Locke had turned against him. What if others in the country lined up against him, too? What if their sympathies were on Moffit's side?

Maybe the next step he ought to take was to make sure their sympathies didn't line up on Moffit's side. It ought to be easy enough if he started right away. Not a one of them but what owed Kennebeck something. Not a one but what would be hurt if he wanted to see him hurt. They depended on him to sell them winter hay and they couldn't get by without it. They depended on him for their summer range and they'd be hurt if he took it away from them. Most of them owed him money, too.

Besides that, Lew's presence meant a loss for them, even if Kennebeck let them strictly alone.

Lew intended to fence his land, and, if he did, several hundred acres of good hay land would be closed to his neighbors' cattle herds.

Kennebeck crossed to the corral and roped himself a horse. He saddled and rode out, heading upcountry. He'd see Roark and McAllister first. After that he'd ride past the Moffit place and see a few of the smaller ranchers who lived beyond. The Slades, the Rossiters, and Emilio Chavez. If all of them would get together and prevent Lew from fencing his land, he'd have to leave, that was all. He couldn't stay because he couldn't live unless he raised some hay.

Kennebeck grinned suddenly to himself. A man alone can only build so much fence in a day. Several other men—they could destroy all he had done and more each night. Best of all, Kennebeck himself wouldn't be involved. Locke couldn't say he was responsible.

He reached the McAllister place, beginning to feel better about Moffit already.

Will Locke rode into Lew Moffit's place a little before noon. He stopped at the house and accepted the coffee Lew offered him. Lew had a pot of beans simmering on the stove. He ladled two plates full and sat down across the table from the sheriff. "Biscuits will be ready in a minute, Sheriff. Meantime, start on those beans."

He watched the sheriff begin to eat hungrily.

When the biscuits were done, he got them out of the oven and put them on the table. He asked: "What happened?"

"Kennebeck wanted you thrown in jail. But his daughter told her story like you said she would and I turned him down."

Lew nodded.

"You're right about Kennebeck. He'll get you any way he can. I warned him but it won't do any good."

"What about Sara? Is she all right?"

"Was when I left. She's his daughter, Moffit, and she's a woman grown. He won't hurt *her*."

"No. I don't suppose he will."

"But he'll hate you even more than he did before. Now he'll blame you for turning Sara against him."

Lew shrugged.

Locke peered closely at him. "What are *you* going to do?"

"Fix the fence. Raise a little hay if I can. Most of the ranchers around here buy at least part of their hay. Kennebeck's been supplying it, but he doesn't raise enough for all of them. I'll sell hay for a few years and buy cattle with what I get for it."

"If he'll let you."

Lew nodded.

"You don't seriously think he will?"

"No, I don't."

"And what, then?"

"I'll fight him."

Locke got up. He stuck out his hand. "I don't think you've got much chance, but I wish you luck."

He went out, mounted, and rode slowly toward the creek. Lew saw him climb his horse out on the other side and head up through the benches along the short-cut route to Glen Cañon, the county seat.

Lew's horse was grazing at the end of a picket rope in the hay meadow not far from the house. He walked out, caught him, and led him back to the house. He threw his saddle on and cinched it down. He went into the house, got the money Sara had left, then went out again, mounted, and rode toward town. If he was going to get any fencing done, he'd better get at it right away.

Alternately walking and trotting his horse, he arrived in town late in the afternoon. He went first to the livery stable and put up his horse, leaving instructions that the animal be grained. He hired a wagon and team, got up on the seat, and drove to the Kennebeck Mercantile, taking a route that avoided the scaffold at the foot of First.

He puzzled briefly at that, at the motives that prompted him to avoid the sight of it. He wasn't afraid of it—he thought he wasn't, at least. But he couldn't be blamed for avoiding it, for it had taken the lives of his father and brother. He'd had an unpleasant experience with it himself not many days before. Besides, looking at it revived his hatred for Kennebeck to a point where he no longer cared about fencing or raising hay—only for revenge, and he was experienced enough to know that revenge is destructive and begets only bitterness.

He went inside. To the right of the door, a middle-aged, bespectacled man was showing yard goods to a young woman and a girl of about ten. Lew walked past them toward the rear of the store.

Another man came forward to wait on him, a man he didn't know and who must have come to town in the ten years he had been gone. The man's eyes were evasive and he seemed excessively pale, so Lew knew he had been recognized.

He said: "I need about forty rolls of wire and a couple of kegs of staples. Want me to drive the wagon around back and load them up?"

The man shook his head. "We don't have any wire on hand right now, Mister Moffit. Or staples, either, for that matter."

Lew stared at him. The man's hands were shaking and his eyes were terrified. Lew said flatly: "You're a liar, mister, and not a very good one, either."

The man backed away from him. His voice

was shrill as he called to the clerk in the front of the store. "Get the marshal, Mister Norton. I think . . ."

Lew stared at him disgustedly. "Why doesn't Kennebeck do his own dirty work? Won't sell it to me, huh? All right. You won't need the marshal. I'll get the wire some place else."

He stalked out angrily, irritated by the almost shameless relief showing in the faces of both clerks. He climbed up on his wagon seat and drove down the street toward the Lehigh Mercantile, a block farther down the street.

He was edgy as he walked in. The place was much smaller than the Kennebeck Mercantile, and more cluttered. Jake Lehigh was behind the candy counter to the right of the door.

Lew asked: "Has Kennebeck got to you, too, Mister Lehigh?"

Lehigh was swarthy and stocky and about seventy years old. But he still looked strong enough to load hundred-pound kegs all day. He nodded reluctantly. "He's got a mortgage on this place, Lew, and it's coming up for renewal next month. I got no choice. Why don't you go on down to Glen Cañon for what you want? Kennebeck can't stop you from getting it there."

Lew nodded. "Guess I'll have to."

He turned to go out, but stopped when Jake Lehigh said: "Good luck, Lew."

He glanced at the storekeeper in surprise. There was something in the man's expression and in his eyes—friendliness, maybe encouragement. He grinned unexpectedly. "Thanks, Mister Lehigh. Thanks."

He went out, feeling better than he had for several days. Kennebeck was giving him all the trouble he could manage, but maybe everyone didn't sympathize with what Kennebeck was doing. Maybe a few of the townspeople were sympathetic toward Lew instead.

He climbed up on the wagon seat and drove out of town, taking the road to Glen Cañon. The sun was dropping behind the ridges to the west and he knew he'd be driving all night or most of it.

There was a certain peacefulness about driving along in the creaking wagon behind the plodding team. He felt more relaxed than he had since coming home.

But he couldn't dodge, in his thoughts, the certainty that there could be no peaceful solution to his difficulties with Kennebeck. Kennebeck would never give up, and sooner or later, Lew was going to have to fight. How it would come out, he couldn't guess. Kennebeck had a tremendous advantage over him. He had money and influence and he was firmly entrenched in the country, enough so that he could make most of its inhabitants do what he told them to. Lew's experience of trying to buy wire in Kennebeck was evidence of that.

Furthermore, Lew knew how easy it would be for Kennebeck to have his new fence destroyed as fast as he built it. And if Kennebeck did that—he'd have no recourse but to fight back or admit defeat and leave.

The brilliant colors of sunset flamed briefly in the west, then faded before the creeping gray of dusk. A star winked, another, and suddenly the sky was black and dotted with stars. A breeze stirred and grew cool, and the horses began to trot steadily along the dusty road.

The hours slipped away and the crescent moon set below the mountains. Lew found his thoughts dwelling on Sara Kennebeck. How long would it be before he could marry her? Would her father ever permit it, and how could he stop it even if he wanted to?

Discouragement touched Lew's thoughts. He knew Kennebeck. And he knew Kennebeck would never permit a Moffit to marry Sara. He would go on fighting until either he or Lew was dead. And even if Lew won, he'd lose, because Sara could never marry the man who was responsible for her father's death.

Troubled and torn with indecision, Lew decided there was only one way he could live his new life here. He'd have to take a single step at a time and live each day separately. To worry about what Kennebeck might do tomorrow would be extreme foolishness.

He drove into Glen Cañon an hour before dawn, watered his team, and took them to the livery barn for a feed of hay. He sat down outside in the darkness to wait for day to break.

XI

Lew had his wire and staples loaded a little after 8:00. He paid for them and climbed to the seat. He drove the heavy wagon out of town, taking the road toward Kennebeck.

He sat, relaxed and comfortable, on the hard, jolting wagon seat. The team plodded ahead of him and he didn't try to hurry them. Getting to Kennebeck was going to take most of the day. It would be after dark before he got home.

Driving a wagon on a long haul gave a man plenty of time to think. He thought of his father, remembering his father's quick, restless way of moving, the sometimes reckless light in his eyes. No wonder his mother had preferred him to Kennebeck. He thought of his father mounting the scaffold steps, knowing he was innocent of the crime for which he was being hanged.

That must have been very hard—to die well when you know the dying is wrong and that you are being punished for another's crime. But Lew suspected, from small things he remembered out of the past, that his father had never really savored life after his wife had died.

And Jess . . . Jess had also mounted those steps for a crime he had not committed. He had died well, as his father had. But both of them must have died hating bitterly, knowing that in some way Kennebeck was behind it all.

If there was hating to be done, he thought, it should all be on the Moffit side. The Moffits were the ones who had been wronged, not Kennebeck. Yet given the chance, Lew believed he would have buried hate, would have buried what had grown into a burning need for vengeance.

The miles slid slowly behind the creaking, slow-moving wagon. He stopped occasionally at some small stream running south to join the river from its source on the high plateau and watered the team.

Hard, back-breaking work lay ahead of him, he realized. Even if Kennebeck let him alone. There was the fencing first, a monstrous job for a man alone. Then there would be ditch work and irrigating and repairs to haying machinery that had been sitting out, rusting and rotting in the weather for the past ten years. After that there was the haying itself, not so hard if a man had help, but Lew knew he would have no help. He'd have to cut it a small patch at a time, rake it, and stack it himself before it spoiled.

At any point along the way, Kennebeck might ruin him. He might prevent the building of the fence by cutting the wire Lew had strung each night. He might burn Lew out, or destroy his haying equipment. He might find some way to deny him water for irrigating or he might wait and burn Lew's stacks after he had them up.

At noon, he was a little more than halfway to Kennebeck. He stopped to let the horses rest and got a drink for himself from a tiny stream. Among other things he was going to have to start eating regularly. He was hungry now, but he had no food.

The afternoon wore slowly away as the morning had done. At about 2:00 he brought the cañon of Hangman's Creek into sight.

Here, the road took an upward trend to avoid rough country lying between Lew and the town. It climbed, angling across a ridge jutting down from the foot of the plateau, and became a shelf road scarcely wider than the wagon itself.

For some reason, a certain tension began to grow in Lew. He wondered if Kennebeck would try to prevent him from reaching home with the wagon and its load.

As if in answer to his question, half a dozen mounted men suddenly appeared on the road ahead of him, coming around a bend behind which they had been concealed.

He started to reach for his gun, but stopped

suddenly. He'd have no chance at all against six men. Besides, he wasn't even sure yet they were hostile.

He recognized none of them but that wasn't surprising in view of the length of time he had been gone. He pulled the wagon as close to the edge of the road as he could to allow them to file on past.

Three of them did, but the other three remained in front of him. One of them asked: "Where you think you're goin'?"

Kennebeck hadn't wasted any time, thought Lew. These were his men; he was sure of it now. There was none of the friendly disinterest there would have been if they had been strangers simply riding along the road.

He said harshly: "Get out of the way. I'm coming through."

The speaker laughed. "Think again, Moffit. You ain't going any place."

Lew felt his anger rising, anger at being helpless in the face of superior odds, anger because he thought he knew what the six had in mind. They intended to see that he didn't reach Kennebeck. They intended to dump his wagon and wire over the edge of this high-shelf road.

But damn them, they were going to have to kill him before they did—and they would have to face the consequences if they did that. Will

Locke had about enough of Kennebeck's high-handedness.

Yelling suddenly at the team, he stood up and slapped their backs with the reins. Startled, they plunged ahead.

They crowded the three back for an instant, and it appeared, briefly, that Lew might get the wagon past. Then the three recovered and closed ranks and one leaped to the ground and seized the bridles of the team, one in each hand, dragging them to a halt.

Standing, the reins in his left hand and his right hand free, seeing the three ahead of him temporarily demoralized, Lew knew he had a better chance right now than he'd ever have again. He snatched at his holster for his gun.

Scarcely had it cleared than a gun blasted behind him. He felt his leg give way and felt himself falling to the road beside the wagon.

He struck the rocky, dusty road, instantly aware of the nearness of the rear wagon wheel. If that passed over him . . .

He rolled, immediately conscious of excruciating pain in his left thigh. The huge, iron-tired wheel ground past him, brushing his shoulder with its nearness as it did.

There was a sudden, warm wetness of blood along the side of his thigh. Damn them! Damn them . . . !

He fought to his feet, realizing that he had lost

his gun in the fall. The wagon was past now, and one of the three who had been ahead of it leaped from his saddle to the wagon seat, snatching up the reins as he did.

Lew spotted his gun and lunged toward it but his leg gave way a second time, and he sprawled just short of it. He tried to crawl, but the gun behind him blasted a second time and the bullet kicked up a shower of dust between Lew's outstretched hand and the gun. It ricocheted off into the empty distances below the road.

Lew froze and turned his head. The gun in the rider's hand was centered squarely on him. The man was grinning as he said: "Sure. Grab it. Go ahead."

Lew raised himself by using the rocks at the side of the road to pull himself erect. He glowered furiously at the riders in the road. The one on the wagon seat was whipping up the team. Lew watched in horror as he deliberately drove too close to the edge and put a rear wheel over it.

The man abandoned the wagon as it tilted dangerously. The rear wheel slid farther off the road until it dragged a front wheel off, too.

The horses, wild with terror, were now fighting furiously. Lunging, straining, squealing with fear, they were gradually pulled to the edge by the heavily loaded wagon. The other rear wheel went off.

There was no chance now, Lew realized as he watched. And then, with a thunderous crash punctuated by the shrill screams of the horses, the wagon went completely over the edge, yanking the horses off in a tangled mass of flying legs, of splintering hardwood, of emptying rolls of barbed wire and kegs of staples. Wagon and horses disappeared from Lew's view to be replaced by a billowing cloud of dust.

But the sound did not fade. Rolling over and over, the wagon tumbled down the precipitous slope until it crashed on the valley floor with a final, thunderously splintering sound.

There suddenly were no sounds at all, save for those slight ones made by the fidgeting horses of the six on the rocky shelf road, save for Lew's own harsh and painful breathing.

He glared at them helplessly. "You bastards! You dirty . . . !"

One of them spurred his horse. The animal's shoulder slammed into Lew. He was flung back, against the rocky wall on the uphill side of the road. With the breath knocked out of him, he stood there fuming, unable for the moment even to speak.

The man who had bowled him back said angrily: "Watch your tongue, Moffit, or you'll follow the wagon down there." He turned his head. "Come on. Let's get out of here."

The six whirled their horses in the narrow road

and thundered away, heading back toward the town of Kennebeck.

Lew sat down helplessly, suddenly overcome by weakness. With his back against the rock wall of the shelf road, he cursed, steadily and helplessly, for several long moments before he stopped.

Kennebeck held all the cards in this game he was playing with Lew. Lew didn't have a chance to win the pot, or even to stay in the game.

Anger burned steadily in his mind, not the towering, flaring anger he had felt while the six were here, but a quieter, more deadly kind. Combined with his innate stubbornness, this anger would stay with him, glowing like a bed of coals, never dying from this day on. Kennebeck had better kill him now. He had better kill him while he could.

He got up painfully and, picking up his gun where it still lay, hobbled to the edge of the road. He stared down at the bodies of the two mangled horses, at the matchwood wreckage of the wagon, at the scattered, partially unwound and tangled rolls of wire. Very little of the wire would even be usable now. Scarred by rocks, it would be too weak to stand stretching in a fence. The staple kegs were not even in sight but he could see the gleam of staples all the way down the slope.

He was wiped out. The money was gone and so was the wire it had bought. But he wasn't giving up. Not yet.

Across the valley he could see a small frame house and the narrow two-track road that led to it from the town of Kennebeck. It was the closest place he might get help. He'd never make it home. Warm blood was seeping steadily from his wound. If it kept bleeding, he would lose what strength was left to him.

He eased himself carefully over the edge of the road and began, carefully and laboriously, to descend to the valley floor below.

It was slow and painful going and he was forced to favor his left leg for fear it would give out on him. Movement increased the bleeding. The bright April sun beat steadily against him. Dust raised when he occasionally slid helplessly for several feet.

His head began to whirl long before he reached the bottom of the slope. Weakness came over him in waves. Pain in his leg was like the searing touch of a branding iron.

Fifty feet from the bottom he lost his footing and his grasp upon the rocks he was using to steady himself and toppled downward. Rolling, banging cruelly against rocks and brush, he tumbled the rest of the way, coming to rest amidst the wagon's wreckage.

He lay quite still for a long time, breathing but

otherwise motionless. Then his eyes came open and stared at the bright blue sky above.

Comprehension dawned in them, and remembrance of what had happened earlier. With it came the slow-burning anger, the stubbornness, the determination to go on.

Even more painfully now than before, he picked himself up and began to stagger almost blindly across the sagebrush-covered valley floor toward the lone ranch house.

XII

Lew Moffit did not remember afterward all of that endlessly long walk to the nearby ranch house. He fell often, from pain and weakness. He crawled sometimes. Sagebrush and gulches blocked his path, but he never stopped moving.

The sun traveled slowly and deliberately down the sky and dropped behind the horizon, afterward staining a few high clouds with its afterglow. In the last of this afterglow, Lew stumbled into the bare yard of the ranch house.

He headed toward the well not far from the back door. He leaned on the pump when he reached it, lacking the strength in this moment to work the pump handle enough to get himself a drink.

The back door opened and a woman came out

211

into the yard, carrying a milk pail. She saw him immediately and the pail clattered on the ground.

For several moments she stared at him fearfully, then came running across the yard. "You're hurt!"

He licked his dry, cracked lips, unable to speak. She worked the handle of the pump and stuck a dipper beneath the spout. She held it to his lips and he drank thirstily.

She was a middle-aged, dried-up woman with her graying hair drawn severely back from her face to form a bun on her neck. She said: "Let me help you into the house. You must have lost a lot of blood. What happened?"

"Shot . . . I . . ." Lew gave up. His thoughts did not seem coherent and he sensed that his speech would be as incoherent as his thoughts.

He leaned on her heavily as she helped him toward the house. He nearly fell going in, but recovered and stood, staring around the room.

There were windows on all four walls and from this he numbly surmised that there were no other rooms. One side of the room contained a bed, the other side the kitchen stove and cupboards for dishes and foodstuffs. The center of the room was taken up by a huge table and a number of chairs.

The woman said: "Come and lie down. I'll . . ."

Lew protested weakly: "My leg . . . the blood . . ."

"Never mind that. You lie down and I'll fetch my husband. He'll know what to do."

Lew crossed the room and sank onto the bed gratefully. The room whirled before his eyes. He closed them but his head continued to whirl. He opened his eyes and shook his head impatiently, trying unsuccessfully to clear it. The woman went out, leaving the door ajar.

Lew stared at the ceiling and waited for her to return.

She was not gone long, and, when she did return, a man was with her, a man older than she with a seamed face and deep-set eyes. He came across the room and stared down at Lew, his face showing no particular expression, neither sympathy nor lack of it. He turned and crossed the room. When he returned, he had a bottle with about two inches of whiskey in the bottom. He raised Lew's head and poured a generous drink into his mouth.

Lew choked and coughed, then let his head fall back. In a state of partial awareness, he heard the man getting a pan and hot water from the stove. He felt his trousers being unfastened and pulled down around his knees. He felt the burn of hot water and soap upon the wound.

There was the sound of tearing cloth, then the feel of its coolness upon his leg. And lastly, there was the strong reek of whiskey and its burn as the man emptied the bottle on the bandage, soaking it.

Lew's trousers were pulled up and refastened. He heard the man say: "Let him alone now. He'll go to sleep."

He heard them moving about within the house for a short time before he dropped off into a state that was partly sleep, partly unconsciousness.

How long he lay this way he could not have said. It was still dark when he awakened. The man was bending over him, shaking his shoulders roughly and saying: "Damn you, wake up! You've got to go. Right now!"

Lew opened his eyes, shocked into partial awareness by the man's roughness and urgency. He mumbled: "What the hell . . . ?"

"You can't stay here, mister. You get up and get out of here."

Lew fought to a sitting position. The room reeled before his eyes. The woman was sitting at the table and her face showed signs of recent tears. She refused to look at him.

Lew thought he understood. He croaked: "Kennebeck's been here, huh?"

The man nodded dumbly. Lew tried to get up, failing until the man helped. He stood swaying for several moments before he started for the door. He asked: "Can you let me have a horse?"

"No! Just get out. Just get out of here and leave us alone."

The man helped him strap on his gun belt before Lew stepped outside into the cool night air. He limped across the yard, hearing the door slam shut behind him.

He stopped, turned, and stared back at it. Weakness came and went in waves, until anger began to smolder in his mind. He turned and headed for the corral. If they wouldn't give him a horse, he'd take one. Without a horse, he'd never make it back to town.

He reached the corral, stopped with his hand upon the gate. If he took a horse from here after being explicitly refused . . . This was the kind of thing Kennebeck wanted him to do. This was what Kennebeck was waiting for.

He turned from the corral and stumbled to the barn. He fumbled around in the scrap lumber piled beside it until he found a board that would serve him as a crutch. Using it to support his wounded leg, he hobbled out of the yard and along the road toward town.

It was hard going, and slow. His mouth grew dry. His leg ached continually and excruciatingly, from ankle to hip. He felt more alone than ever before in his life. He felt as though every man's hand was against him.

He gritted his teeth and went on. His leg was bleeding again, soaking the bandage and his trousers over it.

But his anger burned on steadily, and perhaps

it was this anger that made it possible for him to go on. Even so, he had to stop and rest often and each time it was a little harder to get up and continue than it had been before.

He began to count his steps silently to himself. He immersed his mind in memories, of his childhood, of his father and Jess, of his years away from here, and lastly of Sara Kennebeck.

The lights of the town ahead took him completely by surprise. He stopped and stared unbelievingly, wondering if this was hallucination or reality.

The lights winked at him, unceasingly, and at last he grinned faintly and moved toward them once again.

He came into Kennebeck Street at its lower end, swung over to First and eventually reached the livery barn where he had left his horse. Judging from the state of activity within the town, he judged it was close to midnight or perhaps a little after it.

Breathing hard, he leaned against the wall of the livery barn. More than anything else he wanted to sit down and go to sleep.

But there could be no rest for him tonight—not until he reached home. If he rested, he wouldn't reach it at all. He'd stay right here.

He pushed himself away from the wall and went through the open doors, up the short plank ramp, and into the livery barn. There was a lantern suspended from a beam overhead that threw a flickering light fifteen or twenty feet back into the cavernous place. On his right was the tack room and office. Inside it, another lantern burned.

He opened the door and staggered inside. The liveryman was sitting in a swivel chair with his feet up on the desk. He opened his eyes and his feet came down. "For God's sake, what happened to you?"

"Shot. Get my horse for me, will you?"

He remembered the liveryman vaguely from his boyhood days. He'd never known the man but he had seen him often in town. His name was Schuler and everybody called him Dutch.

"Your horse? Where's my wagon and team?"

Lew said: "Talk to Kennebeck about that. One of his men put it over the edge just outside of town."

"Kennebeck? I'll talk to you about it, mister. I hired it to you. That team and wagon was worth three hundred bucks."

Lew said wearily: "It's gone. The wagon's wrecked and the horses are dead. With it are two hundred dollars' worth of barbed wire and staples."

Schuler's face began to turn red. There was sweat on his forehead. "By God, I'll have the law on you. You walk in here calm as you please and tell me my wagon's gone. But I don't hear you offerin' to pay for it."

Lew said irritably: "Get the law on me if that's what you want to do. But right now get my horse."

"Ha! Like hell I will. I'll just keep that horse until I'm paid. That's what I'll do. And what do you think you're going to do about it, huh?"

For an instant Lew was silent. He felt beat and more weary than he ever had in his life.

Schuler wasn't through. His voice raised until it was almost a screech. "That ain't all I'll do, either! I'll go down to the county seat and I'll slap a lien on that ranch of yours, that's what I'll do. I'll tie you up so tight you can't make a move!"

Lew's anger was growing, like coals fanned by a sudden breeze. Schuler screeched: "Now get out of here! Get out! I don't want nothin' to do with the likes of you! Not ever!"

Lew tried to keep his voice calm, but there was a dangerous edginess about it all the same. He said: "I asked you to get my horse. I'll ask just once more."

"All right, you ask once more. You ask a thousand times and you'll still get the same damn' answer out of me. No! I'll give you the same no a thousand times!"

Lew shifted his position slightly and pulled his

revolver from its holster. He cocked the hammer deliberately.

Schuler's eyes dropped to the gun, then raised to stare into Lew's eyes. Lew said evenly: "I don't want to do this, but you don't give a man much choice. And don't think I'm bluffing, either, mister. I've been pushed and kicked and knocked around ever since I got back here. I've been shot twice and damned near hanged. I'm going to ride out of here on my horse and you're either going to be alive when I do or you're going to be dead. You decide which it's going to be and decide right now."

The flush was gone from Schuler's face. His eyes were suddenly pinched and scared. He stared fixedly at the gun in Lew's hand and nodded violently. "I'll get him."

He started to go past, but Lew put out a hand and halted him. "Take the lantern. And move slowly, mister. I can't run but I sure as hell can shoot."

Schuler picked up the lantern, his hand shaking. He went out the door and Lew followed him. Schuler shuffled along with deliberate slowness and Lew stayed close behind.

The liveryman got Lew's horse out of a stall and led him to the front of the livery barn. He got Lew's saddle and bridle from the tack room.

When the horse was ready, Lew said: "Now give me a hand up."

He kept the gun in his hand all through the awkward procedure. Then he holstered it and rode out into the street. He had gone no more than a block before he heard Schuler yelling breathlessly: "Marshal! I've been robbed! I've been robbed!"

He rode through town and out of it, grinning wryly to himself.

XIII

Lew discovered, before he had even left the town, that riding with his wounded leg was at least as painful as walking on it, using a crutch for support. Every step the horse took jolted him, and, because the leg was hurt, he was unable to use the stirrup for support as he normally would have done.

But at least he covered the ground much more quickly on a horse. He left the town behind and started up the valley of Hangman's Creek.

The wound in his leg was only a flesh wound and the bullet had passed cleanly through, hitting neither artery nor bone. He had been weakened by it and knew it would be painful for a matter of weeks. But it had been taken care of as well as it could have been and it would not incapacitate him for getting around at least. Working would be impossible.

Not that there was any work he could do. His wire and staples were gone. So was the money Sara had left for him to buy them with.

However he tried not to face the fact, he realized that Kennebeck had all but beaten him. He was broke and, unless the fence could be repaired, had no chance of earning anything.

He could survive for a while by eating game. But sooner or later, unless he could borrow against the ranch, he would have to give up and leave.

In the darkness his eyes were hard, his mouth firm and determined. He'd stay as long as he could. He wouldn't leave until he was forced to leave.

Kennebeck's house and ranch yard were dark when he rode past them, except for a single light inside the house. He wondered if Sara was still up, wondered if she knew what had happened today. He doubted if she did, believing she would have found him and helped if she had.

The sky was completely dark and there were no clouds. The air was clear and the stars shone brightly. The road, at the upper edge of Kennebeck's place, ascended steeply as it crossed a jutting ridge. Just before he reached the top, Lew saw a reddish glare in the sky ahead.

It was a couple of seconds before he realized what it was. When he did, he kicked his horse into a jolting trot and a few moments later reached the summit of the ridge.

There could no longer be any doubt. The fire was at his own place. Though he was still several miles away, he could see that the house was all but completely consumed and that the barn was blazing brightly. Several smaller buildings also appeared to be burning, eliminating any possibility that the fire could have been an accident.

Not satisfied with destroying Lew's fence supplies, not satisfied with having him shot, Kennebeck had now fired his ranch. He had done, tonight, everything he could to Lew, short of killing him.

Lew kicked the horse into a run. Swaying dangerously back and forth in his saddle, clinging to the horn for support, he thundered along the road toward his ranch. His forehead broke out in beads of sweat. His face turned white and tense with strain.

He reined in at the lane and thundered down toward the house. A hundred feet away from it he stopped, slid off the horse, and tied him to a post. He hobbled across the yard toward the house.

He stopped while but a dozen yards from it. The heat was so great he could go no closer. He raised a hand to shield his eyes, then backed away, a reluctant step at a time.

Stunned and numb, both with pain and shock, he backed as far as the woodpile and sat down upon a block. He let his head drop into his hands.

He could see no hope now. He could see no chance to win. All that was left to him was his land and his life, which, in his wounded condition, he would scarcely be able to sustain.

He couldn't work, even if anyone would give him a job. He had no place to sleep except in the open. And he knew Kennebeck wasn't through with him. Not yet.

He glanced up again at the burning house as a wall collapsed thunderously, sending up a towering column of sparks and flame. His father had built that house. He had been born there and so had his brother Jess. It held all his childhood memories and now it was suddenly gone, reduced to a pile of charred timbers and glowing coals.

His eyes narrowed. Kennebeck had done all these things to him and what had he done to Kennebeck? Nothing. But that was going to change. If he had to sleep in the open, it didn't matter where. If he was going to live off the land, he could do it as easily on the move as he could right here.

He might be beaten, but he wasn't going to quit. Not until Kennebeck had paid for the things he had done to him. Not until Kennebeck had paid as well for what he had done to Lew's father and to his brother Jess. If ever a man had cause for vengeance, Lew had it now.

Beating down his anger determinedly, he considered the alternatives to the course he had all but chosen for himself. He could mount his horse and leave the country tonight, never to return. He could wait until morning, or until Sara rode up here again and then he could take her with him and leave. Except that if he did, Kennebeck would never rest until he had found them, killed Lew, and forced Sara to return with him.

The third alternative was the only one he found palatable. He could return some of the viciousness Kennebeck had shown him since he came back a week ago. He could take the offensive against Kennebeck, attacking and running and attacking again. He could make Kennebeck wish he'd never heard the name Moffit. He could make him wish he had left Lew strictly alone.

He was tired and weak, but, if he was going to attack Kennebeck, he had better do so tonight.

He got up and walked to his horse. He mounted with difficulty but for the moment he held the horse completely still. If he followed the course he had chosen, it would make an outlaw of him. Not only Kennebeck would be hunting him. The sheriff would be hunting him with a posse, too. Perhaps in the end he would mount the scaffold steps just as his father and brother had done. And Sara would be forever lost to him.

But he could see no other way. He wasn't going to leave. There was no good reason why he should.

He walked the horse toward the creek, turning south when he reached its banks. He headed toward Kennebeck's place unhurriedly, not wanting to reach it until the early morning hours when everyone would be asleep.

It was slow going and very painful for him. Several times he stopped, dismounted, and lay down on the ground. The creek tumbled along, making its familiar roar, and the air grew chill. There was a smell in the air, of earth stirring with spring growth, of green things sprouting, a moist, pleasant smell that Lew had always liked. And over it all was the ever-present, pungent smell of sage.

Lew let his mind wander without direction. He remembered his father, quick-smiling, quick to anger, and as quick to forget whatever it was that had angered him. He remembered the awful night they had come after him, and the loneliness afterward.

Jess had become a father to him after that and had tried to fill the gap caused by their father's death. But it hadn't been the same. It could never be the same.

There was another night Lew would never

forget—the night they came after Jess. And not long afterward, Lew was alone in the world.

He remembered sharply his own terror at leaving all the familiar things that were home and riding away alone. Only fifteen at the time, he'd known he couldn't stay. Perhaps he had sensed that Kennebeck was behind all the troubles the Moffit family had experienced. Or perhaps he'd only known that someone was.

He passed the halfway point between Kennebeck's place and his own and glanced up at the sky. It was after midnight now. If he continued at his present pace, he should reach Kennebeck's at about 2:00.

He plodded along, sitting slightly sideways in the saddle to spare his wounded leg. There were times when weakness made his head whirl, when he had to cling to the saddle horn. The weakness always passed, though he was never without the pain.

At last he reached the place he had stopped a couple of days ago when he'd delivered Lane Yost's body to Kennebeck. He reined in his horse, listening to the night noises in the air, the ever-present roar of the tumbling creek, the rustle of wind in the trees, the stirring of horses in Kennebeck's corral. Then he urged his horse into motion and rode up the narrow road toward the ranch yard.

Kennebeck might have a man on guard but he

doubted it. The man was too arrogant to expect Lew to retaliate. Maybe that was the trouble. None of the Moffits had ever retaliated before.

At the edge of the yard he dismounted and tied his horse. Limping, he crossed the yard afoot.

A dog came rushing at him, barking. He cursed it softly, and it approached, wagging its tail. He put out a hand and briefly scratched its head. With the dog following him, he continued toward the barn.

The doors squeaked as he entered. He searched around blindly for several minutes, looking for a can of kerosene. The dog sat in the doorway and scratched. Failing to find it, Lew climbed the ladder to the loft and, with his arms, raked down a huge pile of hay, a pile high enough almost to reach the floor of the loft above.

Uneasy about the noise he had made, he climbed back down the ladder and went to the door. The yard was still empty, still silent.

Lew crossed to the corral, the dog following. He went in and for several moments looked over the horses carefully. After selecting the one that looked the best, he took a rope from the corral gate and threw out a loop. The horse quieted immediately and Lew led him out the gate. He walked across the yard, unsaddled his own animal, and turned him loose. He put saddle and bridle on the fresh horse, then led him across the yard to the open doors of the barn.

Holding the reins of the stolen horse, he stepped into the door opening and struck a match. He threw it into the pile of dry hay and watched it catch. He waited until the flames reached the loft, then turned and mounted his horse. Riding slowly, he left the yard by the lane leading up to the road.

He climbed the horse twenty or thirty yards into the cedars and dismounted again. He tied the reins to a tree, pulled his rifle from the saddle scabbard, and sat down to wait.

There was already a glow in Kennebeck's yard from the open doors of the barn. The dog began to bark.

A light gleamed inside the bunkhouse and a few moments later a man came out the door, wearing only his underwear and carrying a lantern. Immediately he began to yell excitedly.

More men poured from the bunkhouse door. Lamps gleamed from the windows of the house.

Still wearing only underwear and boots, the crew began to gather buckets and form a fire line between the barn and the pump. Grinning slightly with satisfaction, Lew shifted position, raised his rifle, and braced his elbows against his knees.

The fire and the glow it threw over the entire yard lighted his sights perfectly by silhouetting them against the glare. He took a careful bead on the well and fired.

He heard the bullet strike, that sound coming solidly upon the heels of the reverberating report. And he saw them stop as though temporarily frozen, saw their faces turn toward him.

He jacked in another cartridge and fired carefully again. The second bullet also struck the well, this time ricocheting off the cast-iron pump with a sound almost like that of a clapper striking a bell.

The men in the yard scattered immediately, seeking cover. Lew heard Kennebeck's voice roaring angrily at them but they did not come out.

Kennebeck himself, unmistakable because of his bulk, shambled across the yard and began to work the pump. The light in the yard was much brighter now and flames were licking out of the upper loft door, seeking out the roof. Kennebeck continued to work the pump and fill buckets, but none of his crew came out to help. He carried one of the buckets toward the barn and flung the contents inside the doors, but Lew knew it was too late now. A hundred men couldn't stop the fire after it had burned this long.

Perhaps the men down there couldn't have put it out even if Lew hadn't stopped them from trying to. Perhaps his bullets had only been for the purpose of letting them know for sure who had been responsible.

Still grinning with a certain fierce pleasure,

Lew went to his horse, shoved the rifle into the scabbard, and mounted painfully. He took one last look at the blazing barn, at the men scurrying around so frantically in the yard. Then he reined his horse upward through the cedars, making no attempt now to hide his trail. They couldn't follow trail at night anyway. And by the time it was light enough for them to trail, he wanted a dozen miles between him and Kennebeck's men.

He reached the narrow trail that ascended the plateau, and began the ascent. He was still in pain, still light-headed at times. Riding was no easier than it had been before.

Yet, for some reason, he felt stronger, surer of himself than he had at any time since his return. He had stopped turning the other cheek. He had struck back and would strike back again. Before he was through, he would be Kennebeck's scourge.

If Kennebeck didn't get him first.

XIV

The trail led upward steadily, but the horse was fresh and strong. Lew kept him moving until he reached the rim.

Here he stopped briefly to rest the horse and stared downward at the scene in Kennebeck's yard, made toy-like by distance.

The bucket line was going in two directions now, between well and house and between well and bunkhouse. Water was being thrown upon the roofs of both buildings to keep them safe from sparks thrown into the air by the blazing barn. As Lew watched, he saw two horsemen leave the yard and head up the lane toward the road.

He understood this move immediately. Kennebeck couldn't spare his entire force because of fire danger to other buildings, but he could spare two. They had been sent to trail Lew as best they could until daylight came. Then one of them would return and lead a larger force to wherever he had left the first. The lantern one carried made a pinpoint of light in the blackness of the valley floor.

Lew urged his horse on up the trail and a few moments later came off the narrow shelf trail onto the plateau top.

He stayed on the main trail leading along the spine of the ridge and lifted his horse to a steady, rocking gallop. It was a hard gait for Lew to ride with his wounded leg, but he didn't dare ride at any slower gait. Besides, a trot would be even worse.

This way, he inched backward along the plateau for half a dozen miles before gray began to touch the eastern sky.

As soon as it did, as soon as he could clearly

231

see the ground, he left the trail and put his horse down onto the slopes between the ridge top and the rim.

Here the quaking aspens were thick in spots and had littered the ground with leaves. He slowed his horse to a walk, making a winding, twisting trail on the soft, dead leaves underfoot.

They would not retain it long, though an expert tracker could follow trail here even after several hours had passed and he had no doubt there was at least one such man in Kennebeck's employ. But if he changed direction often, he would slow even an expert.

Sometimes the aspens gave way to spruces, green and fragrant in the warmth of the rising sun. And sometimes he broke out immediately above the rim and was able to ride on crumbled shale for several miles.

At 7:00, he reached the divide that led from the east side of Hangman's Creek to the western side. Here he stopped, watered his horse in the narrow stream that was the beginning of Hangman's Creek, then got down and took a long, cold drink himself.

He tied the horse securely to the lower limb of a spruce, lay down in the sun, and closed his eyes.

His head whirled, his leg ached abominably, and he felt more tired than he had in a long, long time. He was asleep almost instantly.

A grouse whirring overhead awakened him once. Another time a big buck deer, spooking away from his first sudden glimpse of the tethered horse, awakened him with a start. But he slept again each time and did not finally rouse himself until midmorning came.

Reluctantly he untied his horse and painfully climbed to the saddle again. He continued westward, hiding his trail as best he could.

They wouldn't catch up with him. That didn't worry him. He could make trail in a country like this much faster than even an expert could unravel it.

What did worry him was the possibility that sooner or later Kennebeck was going to stop trying to track him. Then the man would scatter his crew out aimlessly on the chance that one of them would see Lew or cut his trail. It wouldn't happen today, however. It wouldn't happen until Kennebeck realized Lew had no intention of leaving the country yet.

He followed along the rim, hiding his trail when possible. Mostly he stayed out of sight, knowing he might be seen by Kennebeck's men on the opposite rim.

The day wore on slowly. The sun reached its zenith and began its slow descent into the western sky. Sometimes, now, Lew would see Kennebeck's men winding through timber pockets on the other rim. When he did, he would grin slightly to himself, savoring thoughts of Kennebeck's fury at being struck twice in the same day.

The burning torture of his wound forced him to stop several times during the afternoon, but toward sundown the pain of dismounting and mounting again made him discontinue the stops and stay where he was. It was slightly after sundown when he reached the trail immediately above Kennebeck's place and started down.

His head was reeling. Tomorrow he was going to have to find a place where he could rest, where he could sleep. He couldn't go on like this.

He reached the bottom of the trail as dusk blended with darkness, wound slowly through the cedars, and at last reached Hangman's Creek. He splashed across, allowing his horse only a brief drink before pulling up his head.

He did not head straight for the house. Instead, he angled left slightly until he came to a wire gate leading into the hay field above Kennebeck's house.

The haystacks were not very hard to spot. Even in darkness they stood out as blacker masses against the lighter color of growing hay around them.

He selected one about a quarter mile from the house, rode to it, and fired it on the side away from the house.

He did not wait to watch the blaze grow. There

was need for hurry now. Instead, he galloped his horse for the next, gritting his teeth angrily against the mounting pain the horse's motion brought to his wounded leg.

He fired a second, and a third. Then, because the first had become a monstrous torch lighting the whole hay field, he put his horse through the gate and down into the brush that lined the creek.

Swiftly he climbed to one of the benches that looked directly down upon the house. Without leaving the saddle, he pulled his rifle from the saddle boot.

Only half a dozen men ran into the hay field to try to save the stacks. As they appeared, Lew began systematically to fire the rifle, driving them to cover, making them inactive until all three stacks would be beyond saving by anyone.

He fired approximately a dozen rounds, reloading twice. Then, grinning faintly to himself, he turned his horse and urged him upcountry along the trail leading to No Name Creek and the short-cut route to Glen Cañon in the west.

He rode steadily, his only stops an occasional one to rest the horse. Sometimes he closed his eyes and dozed, awakening when he felt himself begin to fall. His thoughts were fuzzy, and pain was his constant companion.

He was only partly conscious when he crossed his own trail, the one he had made heading around the rims earlier, but roused himself enough to study the trail and make sure no one had followed him. Apparently they had not.

He stayed in the saddle all through the night and part of the following day. At last he could go no farther. He had reached the limit of his strength.

Glancing around, he selected a high knob covered with scattered boulders and climbed its side. He slid off the horse at the top, steadying himself by clinging to the saddle afterward. He found a small clump of brush to which he could tie his horse, then staggered back in the direction he had come until he found a vantage point from which he could see the country he had traveled through for several miles.

Leaning his rifle against a rock, he lay down and closed his eyes. Sleep overtook him immediately.

He slept all through that afternoon and all through the night, but it was not an easy sleep. It was tormented with dreams, or rather with a recurring dream in which he was riding down the road to Placerville with the others, intent on robbing the local bank.

Only he did not turn off; he did not leave his companions. He kept going with them and they reached Placerville only to find that instead of a town and a bank, all that awaited them was a looming, grisly scaffold and an angry mob of men.

One by one they were dragged up the steps until at last it was Lew's turn. No matter how he fought, it did no good. Step by step, they dragged him up and at the top put the heavy, knotted noose over his head and tightened it.

In the dream he waited breathlessly for the trap to spring, staring down into the faces of the men beneath. But there was only one face on all of them. It was the heavy, angry, hating face of Kennebeck.

He would awake each time to find himself sweating heavily but chilled all the way to his bones.

Each time he lay awake, staring into the darkness for a while, afraid to go back to sleep, afraid the dream would recur. But he couldn't stay awake and each time he went to sleep the dream began again.

The last time he awoke, it was to find the sun poking above the ridges to the east. He shifted his position slightly so that it beat steadily down on him

He rubbed his eyes and stared groggily down at the trail he had traveled coming here yesterday. He saw nothing. He realized that he felt much stronger and that he was ravenously hungry. He wondered what Kennebeck was doing now. Of one thing he was sure. Every man in Kennebeck's crew would be out this morning combing the country for ten miles around the ranch. They would have orders to shoot Lew Moffit on sight—and to shoot to kill. Probably Kennebeck had also sent for Locke. . . .

Lew got up stiffly. He discovered that, while his wounded leg was exceedingly stiff, the pain was much less than it had been before.

A heavy growth of whiskers covered his jaws. His mouth was dry and cottony. He walked to his horse, untied the reins, and climbed into the saddle. He rode down off the knob, taking a course that would cut the main trail to Glen Cañon.

He rode watchfully, encouraged by the way he felt today. He doubted if Kennebeck's men had come this far. After being hit twice in twenty-four hours, Kennebeck would be keeping most of them close to home, guarding the ranch against further depredations.

Undoubtedly he had sent for Will Locke and a posse. Kennebeck was good at letting the law do his dirty work when all else failed.

He reached the top of the ridge that looked down upon the Glen Cañon trail. There was a small stream in the bottom of the gulch, which the trail crossed and re-crossed repeatedly.

He looked at it longingly, licking his dry lips. He knew it was possible that Locke had already traveled this trail heading for Kennebeck's, but he doubted it. Locke wouldn't hurry himself unduly for Kennebeck. Besides, it takes time to form a posse, supply it, and come this far.

He stayed in his saddle for nearly an hour, watching the gulch below, letting his hungry horse graze. At last he heard, distantly, the unmistakable sound of a man's voice.

Immediately he pulled up his horse's head and rode out of sight into a pocket of brush. Peering through it, he saw Locke and half a dozen men ride into view.

He turned, rode off the ridge on the side away from them. He angled right until he reached the bottom of the gulch in which the Glen Cañon trail was located. He dismounted and tied his horse out of sight in the middle of a thick pocket of scrub oak. Then he stepped to the downcountry side of it and waited, his rifle in his hands.

He could hear them talking as they approached. He saw Locke's horse come into sight, waited until all the other six were plainly in sight as well.

He drew in a deep breath. Locke might be cautiously sympathetic toward him, but holding a gun on Locke and robbing him wasn't going to help his cause.

Yet he knew of nothing else that he could do. He couldn't, didn't dare trust anyone in the valley of Hangman's Creek or in the town of Kennebeck. And he had to have food.

He jacked a cartridge into the rifle audibly. He said in a voice that croaked: "Hold it, Sheriff.

Hold it right there and tell your men to keep their hands off their guns. Nobody will get hurt."

He waited, holding his breath, while Locke halted and stared at him uncertainly.

XV

The wait seemed interminable. Locke's men, behind him, shifted their glances uneasily between Lew and the sheriff. At last Locke said: "Hold it, all of you. I'll take care of this."

Lew's breath sighed out audibly.

Frowning, Locke asked: "What the hell's the big idea? Want to give yourself up?"

Lew laughed shortly. "What do you think, Sheriff? I may be hurt but I'm not crazy."

"Then what do you want?"

"A horse. Some food. Right now, suppose you shuck your gun. Then tell your men to do the same."

Locke stared closely at him a moment, then carefully unbuckled his gun belt and let it fall. He half turned his head. "One at a time, the rest of you. Don't start anything."

The posse members followed suit, one after the other. Lew watched them warily until the last gun belt was on the ground. He said: "Now the rifles."

Locke scowled, but he eased his rifle from the boot and let it fall. The others did likewise.

Lew relaxed slightly. He stared up at Locke. "What did Kennebeck tell you?"

"That you'd fired his barn. That you burned up three of his stacks."

"Did he tell you that he had me shot and my wagon load of wire driven off the road just south of Kennebeck? Did he tell you that he burned every building on my place?"

Surprise showed briefly in the sheriff's eyes. Then they sparkled with anger. "No. He didn't tell me that."

"I didn't think so. Well, he did. I burned his barn and haystacks afterward."

"Ever think of calling in the law?"

Lew laughed harshly. "You're good with the jokes this morning, Mister Locke. Think I could have proved anything? Kennebeck may be crazy but he's not stupid. He and every member of his crew would have been some place else when it happened. There'd be witnesses to say they were. Kennebeck's story would be that I did those things myself to try and get at him. And what would you have said?"

Locke shrugged helplessly. "That I didn't have enough evidence to arrest him, I suppose."

"All right then. I'm just doing it my way. I'm doing it the only way it can be done."

"You'd better let me take you into custody, son.

You'll be dead in twenty-four hours if you don't. You'll get a fair shake. I'll see to that myself."

"The way you saw to it with my father and with Jess? You told me yourself it wasn't your job to decide whether a man was guilty or not. You said that was up to the court."

A stain seeped into the sheriff's face. "What are you going to do, then? How long do you think you can keep going with a hole like that in your leg?"

"As long as I have to. And I'm going to keep hitting Kennebeck. Tell him that. I'm going to keep hitting him until he's in the same fix I am. Broke, and without even a roof over his head."

"You're a fool. Kennebeck's got a twenty-man crew. He's got half the people in the country in his debt. You won't last until this time tomorrow."

"Maybe not. But right now I want a horse from you and a sack of grub. We'll ride on toward Kennebeck's for a couple of miles before I leave you. Then you can come back for your guns."

"All right, son. But you're piling up a lot of counts. You've admitted to arson and you're riding a stolen Kennebeck horse. Before you're through you'll kill somebody. You might make it up that scaffold yet if you keep going the way you are."

Lew shrugged. He said: "I'll take your horse, Mister Locke. Get down and unsaddle him."

Locke dismounted. He removed his saddle and flung it on the ground. Lew slid off his own horse carefully. He said: "Put my saddle on him."

The sheriff complied. He switched bridles after that. When he had finished, Lew untied the gunny sack behind the sheriff's saddle and peered inside. He grinned. "This will do. At least I'll eat." He re-tied the sack behind his own saddle. He mounted awkwardly, discovering that for the first time his leg would bear his weight as he did. He said: "All right. Let's go."

Locke led out and Lew held his horse motionless until the posse members had followed him. There was no visible animosity or anger in any of them. They were taking their cues from the sheriff, and, if Locke didn't intend to resist, obviously none of the posse members did, either. Lew thought he detected a certain friendliness in a couple of them.

It was an encouraging sign but it didn't solve any of his problems for him. So far Kennebeck had only been pricked. He hadn't been really hurt.

Lew followed Locke's posse for a couple of miles. Then, without announcing his departure, he cut away and rode silently north up a narrow, brushy draw. He had gone a quarter mile before, looking back, he saw Locke and his posse returning for their guns.

He stopped shortly afterward. Without dismounting, he untied the sack and withdrew several biscuits and a piece of meat. He ate them ravenously, riding, and soon afterward stopped at a small spring for water. Going on, he felt stronger than he had at any time since he was wounded two days before.

Watchfully he turned his horse and rode toward Hangman's Creek. It would be very dangerous, showing up at Kennebeck's tonight. But the effects of what he had done already would be blunted if he didn't strike again.

On the other hand, if he continued hitting Kennebeck, the man might become sufficiently enraged to do something for which Locke could hold him accountable. He might be the one who mounted the scaffold instead of Lew. He frowned slightly as he rode, wondering which, of all the things he might possibly do, would enrage his enemy the most.

XVI

After two days and nights in her room, Sara Kennebeck was almost beside herself with fear for Lew. She didn't know what had happened, but she had learned from questioning her guards that her father had burned Lew's buildings, destroyed his fencing materials, and had wounded him in the leg.

Lew had retaliated by burning her father's barn and three of his haystacks. Yet she knew that even now he might be lying somewhere out in the brush, feverish and weak from his wound, unable to get away or defend himself if he were found. She knew her father well enough to realize that he wouldn't care whether Lew was well or not when he put the hangman's noose around his neck.

If there were only something she could do . . . but there wasn't. Not as long as she remained a prisoner.

She went to the window and stared down into the yard. Several chickens were scratching in the middle of it. There were two horses in the corral. No smoke issued from the bunkhouse chimney. A single man sat with his back against the bunkhouse wall, a rifle across his knees.

Today, in desperation, Sara was considering something she had never considered before—a physical assault upon her guard in an attempt to get away.

She had gone over every other possible plan in her mind and had discarded them one by one. Her only real attempt to escape by tying strips of her sheet together and sliding down to the ground had been discovered. Now she had no sheets on her bed.

She glanced around the room, her eye lingering on the pitcher of water on the washstand and on a small, three-legged stool. She crossed the room and picked up the pitcher. She put it down and picked up the stool, holding it in both hands by two of its three short legs. It weighed enough, she thought, and her hands began to shake.

She crossed the room to the door and took up a position that would put her behind it when it opened to admit her guard. She bit her lip, trying to calm her shaking nerves. Then, in a voice that was far from natural, she called: "Joe! Come quick!"

She heard the chair he sat on outside in the hall crash to the floor. She heard his approaching footsteps, heard the door flung open. She saw him, saw his back, and the back of his head as he plunged into the room. She swung the stool, which she was holding above her head, with blind force. She felt it strike with a sound that made her sick. Joe pitched forward and fell face downward on the floor. Blood stained his straw-colored hair, seeping slowly from the wound.

She dropped the stool and sank to her knees at his side. She cried: "Joe! Are you all right? Oh, God, I've killed him!"

He groaned softly and she saw that he was breathing regularly. He stirred slightly, trying to roll over.

He wasn't dead, she thought. He was only knocked out. He'd have a headache when he came to and perhaps no job, but he wasn't going to die.

She jumped to her feet and fled out the door. At the head of the stairs she stopped, turned, and ran back to him. She seized his revolver from its holster. Carrying it in her hand, she ran down the stairs and out into the yard.

The man in front of the bunkhouse got up and shambled toward her. She cried hysterically: "Stay right there or I'll shoot!"

He kept coming. She raised the gun and fired into the ground twenty or thirty feet in front of him. He stopped uncertainly.

Sara ran on to the corral and caught herself a horse. She bridled him but did not bother with a saddle. She mounted bareback and headed for the creek.

She splashed her horse across and climbed him through the brush toward the cedars. And now the full difficulties of her undertaking began to present themselves in her mind. If her father and his men couldn't find Lew, how did she expect to find him? And how to evade her father's men while she was searching for him?

She didn't have a chance. But even as she realized this, her small jaw hardened and her lips compressed. Lew hadn't a chance, either, but he hadn't stopped trying because of that. And neither would she stop trying to find and help him all she could.

After that, she climbed her horse steadily toward the brushy slide below the rim. About an hour before noon she reached the foot of it and stopped to rest her horse. There was a trail not far from here leading out on top but it was virtually certain her father would have someone guarding it. And all the other trails leading out on top as well.

Sitting there, she saw a file of horsemen working their way downcountry toward the ranch along the trail that led to Glen Cañon by way of No Name Creek. She stared closely, finally recognizing Sheriff Locke in the lead.

Immediately she put her horse down the slope in front of her and headed for them. Ten minutes later she stopped in the trail to wait.

Locke came riding up out of a draw and drew his horse to a halt ten feet away from her. He touched the brim of his hat. "Howdy, Miss Kennebeck."

"Did my father send for you?"

He nodded.

"Did he tell you all the things he did to Lew Moffit before Lew burned his barn and stacks?"

"He didn't, ma'am, but Lew did."

Sudden, wild excitement touched her. "You've seen him?"

"No more'n a couple of hours back. He took a horse from us and some grub."

"Is he all right?"

"So far. The food'll help him. He's a tough one, Miss Kennebeck. I wouldn't worry about him too much."

"Are you going to arrest him?"

Locke laughed wryly. "Don't look like I'll get the chance. Ain't sure I would even if I could. Your father's gone too far this time, Miss Kennebeck."

"Tell me where you saw him."

Locke grinned at her. "You won't find him there. But try riding along the Glen Cañon trail. Mebbe he'll find you."

"Thank you, Sheriff." She moved her horse aside so that they could pass. One by one the posse men touched their hat brims passing her, or nodded, or ducked their heads in acknowledgment of her presence. Their faces were, without exception, both sympathetic and friendly.

Perhaps, she thought as she went on, her father was losing more ground than he thought. If he lost the support of the country's inhabitants and the support of his crew, he lost his battle with Lew. Encouraged for the first time in many days, she urged her horse along the trail.

XVII

Sitting his horse just at the edge of a heavy clump of oak brush, Lew saw her ride past along the trail and recognized her at once,

His immediate inclination was to ride down and intercept her, but he didn't yield to it. Instead, he sat motionlessly for nearly ten minutes, staring at the trail along which she had so recently passed.

After satisfying himself that she wasn't bait, that no one was following her, he touched his horse's sides with his heels and slid him straight down the steep slope until he reached the trail.

Urging the horse to a gallop, he rode after her. A mile after reaching the trail he overtook her in a small, brushy draw.

She turned her head in startled fright, and her expression changed instantly to one of relief and concern. "Lew! Are you all right?"

"So far. Let's get off the trail."

He led the way up the draw for about a quarter mile. Then he swung from the back of his horse and Sara followed suit. She came to him immediately and he closed her in his arms.

He was conscious of the fact that he had neither shaved nor had clean clothes for several days, but Sara, apparently, did not notice. When she drew away, there were tears in her eyes. "You look so thin. And tired."

"I'm all right."

"I couldn't get away until now, Lew. After I told Sheriff Locke about Lane Yost, Father put me in my room with a guard at the door." She paused breathlessly, then went on: "Lew, I found a picture of your mother in his desk and asked him about it. It sounds crazy, but that's why he hated your father. It's why he hates you. He wanted her and she married your father instead."

Lew whistled soundlessly. "That's where that picture went." He shook his head. "And he's still hating after thirty years."

"What are you going to do now?"

"The only thing I can. I'm going to keep hitting him."

"Maybe you won't have to as long as you think you will. People around here aren't behind him the way they used to be. Mister Locke and the men with him . . . I think they're on your side."

He nodded, his eyes resting steadily on her face.

"Lew, let's go away. Right now. We can go so far he'll never be able to find us."

He shook his head stubbornly. "That isn't the way you talked at first. And you were right. We'd never know. Every time we heard a horse outside the house at night . . . every time we heard there was a stranger in town . . . that's no way to live, Sara. Uhn-uh. This has got to be settled now."

"Lew, please. . . ."

He looked steadily into her eyes. Refusing was the hardest thing he had ever done. But he knew that to run away would be to live out his life in fear. And sooner or later—sometime— Kennebeck had not stopped hating for thirty years. He wouldn't stop now until he was dead. Lew shook his head again.

Her eyes filled with tears. Her lower lip trembled but she whispered resignedly: "All right, Lew. I suppose you're right. But be careful. Promise me?"

"I'll be careful. Now you ride down the trail. Catch up with Locke. Tell him you want to go to Glen Cañon with him. And stay there until I come for you."

She nodded and he supposed she meant she would. He helped her to her horse and watched her ride away. When she had gone a hundred yards, she turned and raised her hand.

Lew mounted and continued up the brushy draw to its head at the foot of the slide. This was as good a place as any to rest and wait for night.

He tied his horse out of sight in the brush and lay down comfortably where he could see the land below.

Once, a couple of Kennebeck's men passed about a mile away and he watched nervously to see if they would discover his trail. Later, a small bunch of cattle wandered past on the slope beneath. Shortly afterward, a doe and twin fawns walked past less than a hundred feet from him.

He stared at the sky, at the drifting clouds. His chance of defeating Kennebeck seemed remote. He frowned, wondering what he could do tonight that would hurt Kennebeck.

And suddenly a pleased smile touched his face. He closed his eyes and dozed, still smiling, while the sun traveled across the sky toward the high ridge to the west.

At 4:00, it threw him into shadow, and at 5:30 disappeared from the valley floor. He could see the shadow of the bluff behind him crawling up the side of the bluff ahead as the sun continued to sink.

He waited until it was deep dusk before he got up and untied his horse. He mounted and threaded his way down through the brush to the Glen Cañon trail.

Here, he could make better time. He crossed through his own place to the road, riding cautiously as always, his ears tuned to each small sound, his eyes watching his horse's head. Usually a horse would hear sound or see someone approaching long before his rider did.

A mile above Kennebeck's place, he left the road and took to the cedars east of it. He stayed in the cedars until he could see the lights of the town ahead.

Again he dismounted. His leg still hurt, but the pain was nothing compared to what it had been before. He wished he had tobacco, but he didn't. He wished he could have a bath, and clean clothes, and a shave, but he knew these things would have to wait.

He waited indolently, watching the lights and the activity below. He saw Kennebeck, followed by four members of his crew, leave the town and head toward home.

He grinned slightly, waited another half hour, then mounted and skidded his horse down the steep, bare slope.

He entered town by way of an alley and stayed in the alley all the way through. He reached First and stopped beneath the scaffold, looming like a grisly skeleton against the sky.

He needed kerosene for this—a lot of it. Leaving his horse tied at the foot of the dark scaffold, he walked up the street until he reached the warehouse of the Kennebeck Mercantile.

Going around to the rear, he smashed a window with the butt of his gun. He climbed on a box and picked the jagged shards of glass out of the window frame. He climbed on through. Breaking and entering had now been added to his list of crimes, he thought wryly, but he opened the back door from the inside and struck a match.

He got two five-gallon cans of kerosene. Carrying them, he went out and returned to the scaffold half a block away.

He put the cans down and untied his horse. He led him across the street and tied him to a rail. Returning, he picked up one of the cans and carried it to the top.

He drenched the platform thoroughly with kerosene. He carried the empty can down, then lugged the other one up. He poured this one equally down each of the four scaffold supports and, when it was empty, carried it down, too.

Limping, he returned to the warehouse. He got a bale of straw from it and carried that back to the scaffold, which now reeked of kerosene. He broke open the bale and scattered loose straw around each of the scaffold supports.

Out of breath, he stopped and fumbled for matches. He struck one and tossed it into a waiting pile of straw. By the time he reached the second and struck the second match, flame was crawling up the kerosene-soaked scaffold support.

He lighted all four piles. Then, quickly, he crossed the street toward his horse.

Only then did he see the dark, silent men that crowded the walk. And seeing them so unexpectedly made a weird, unpleasant chill crawl along his spine.

He snatched out his gun and thumbed the

hammer back. Behind him the flames reached the scaffold platform. The whole thing had grown into a monstrous torch, lighting the entire area for a block around.

Lew reached his horse. No one on the crowded boardwalk moved. Lew didn't understand, but he held his gun ready. No one was going to take him. If he had to, he'd fight the whole damned town.

He could see some of their faces in the growing light, and suddenly he realized that there wasn't an ounce of hostility in the lot of them. They were just watching. Some of their faces even showed their approval of what he had done.

He started to mount and a man stepped forward to help him up. But before he could, another came toward him, leading a horse. The man's voice, recognizable as that of Jake Lehigh, said: "Here's a fresh horse, Lew. There's grub tied on behind. And clean clothes. And a slicker and blankets."

Lew stared at him unbelievingly, wondering if this was some kind of cruel joke.

Jake said: "It's no trick, Lew. And before you ride out, Doc Miles wants you to stop by his place. He says that leg ought to have a clean dressing on it at least."

In the yellowish light from the blazing scaffold, Lew stared around him in bewilderment. Some of these same people, egged on by Kennebeck and his crew, had all but hanged him from that scaffold less than a week ago. Now they were doing this. . . .

He asked, half angrily: "Why? Why the sudden change of heart?"

"They didn't know you a week ago, Lew. They believed what Kennebeck said about you. Now they know it wasn't true. They haven't liked seeing this scaffold standing here all these years. They haven't liked a lot of the things Kennebeck did. Maybe they figure you've taken all you should have to take from Kennebeck." Lehigh grinned sheepishly. "Lew, they're trying to say they're sorry. And so am I."

Lew's voice was hoarse. "All right. Let's go see the doc. Kennebeck will be back as soon as he sees that blaze."

Trying not to limp, he walked up the street beside Jake Lehigh. He climbed the stairs to Doc Miles's office and sat in a chair while Doc changed the bandages. Doc said: "Wound's clean, but you ought to have some rest. If you don't . . ."

"If I do, I might be resting permanently."

Doc Miles grunted by way of reply. Lew pulled up his pants and settled his gun comfortably at his side. He followed Jake outside, went down the stairs, and mounted his horse. At least his wound was clean and was healing properly.

He glanced down at Jake, filled with conflicting feelings. The burning scaffold threw a glow upon the entire town. A horse-drawn fire engine clanged around a corner half a block away, heading for the blaze. Lew asked: "They're going to put it out?"

"Uhn-uh. Just seeing to it nothing else catches from it."

Lew said: "Kennebeck will build a new one tomorrow."

"Then he'll have to do it by himself. Nobody in town is going to help."

Lew started to turn. As he did, Jake said hesitantly: "Lew, in the morning there will be a wagonload of wire at your place."

"I can't . . ."

"Did I say you had to pay for it now? Pay me when you can. If you never pay for it, that's all right, too."

"Jake, I . . ." Lew stared down at him for several moments. Then, wordlessly, he turned his horse and rode away.

It was encouraging to have the people of the town on his side. But he didn't delude himself into thinking it would change anything. He still had Kennebeck to fight. And Kennebeck would never change.

XVIII

Lew picked himself a spot high in the cedars above the town to spend the night. He tied his horse, then walked back to a high point, and stared at the town below. The scaffold was down, was now only a glowing pile of coals.

He shook his head and returned to where he had left his saddle. He removed the bundle of clothes and changed. He spread blankets on the ground and lay down on them. But he did not go to sleep immediately. He stared at the stars instead, puzzling at the sudden change in the attitude of the townspeople. That change would make things easier for him, of course, but it wouldn't change Kennebeck.

He drifted off to sleep, a deep sleep tonight without disturbing dreams. He awoke at dawn, dressed, and ate cold food from the sack behind his saddle. He saddled his horse and checked the loads in his guns. Mounting, he rode back to the high point from which he could see the town.

Though the sun was not yet up, men were already at work, clearing away the ashes and débris left by the burning scaffold. A wagon loaded with timbers waited nearby. Even at this distance, Kennebeck's burly figure was visib' striding back and forth, gesturing and shouti·

Building a new scaffold, thought Lew, *to replace the old.* He turned his horse and, staying in the cedars, rode upcountry toward his own place. He didn't know exactly what he was going to do next. He needed time to think.

The sun was well up in the sky before he reached his place. When he could see it from the cedars, he stopped and stared unbelievingly. There were men down there, a dozen or more of them. There was a wagon, and there were saddle horses and buggies and buckboards. The men were strung out in a line along the road and were rebuilding the fence. Sun reflected from new wire already strung between the burned buildings and the road.

Lew sat motionlessly for a long time, his feelings conflicted and confused. Then he put his horse down through the cedars until he reached the road.

The men glanced up at him and nodded, but did not speak. Roark and McAllister were here, along with McAllister's hired man. So was Luke Slade and Emilio Chavez. The rest were men from town.

Lew dismounted and tied his horse to a fence post. Chavez was struggling with a full roll of wire through which a bar had been thrust to facilitate unrolling it. Lew walked to him and took one end of the bar.

Emilio, dark and quick, grinned at him.

Together, they walked along the fence, unrolling wire as they went.

At noon they stopped when Rose McAllister drove up in a buggy with dinner for them. They sat on the edge of the road and ate. A few kept glancing uneasily down the road toward town, as though expecting momentarily to see Kennebeck and his crew storming into sight.

Emilio Chavez said: "I turned a head of water into your ditch a while ago, Lew. You can start irrigating tomorrow."

"This fence is going to do all of you out of a lot of pasture."

Chavez shrugged. "There is other pasture land."

"It won't make you popular with Kennebeck."

Chavez spat by way of reply. Yet even as he did he glanced uneasily down the road toward town.

Lew knew Kennebeck would come. He'd come as soon as he got the scaffold built.

It was midafternoon, however, before Lew looked up and saw the distant cloud of dust rising about a mile toward town. The others saw it, too, and unobtrusively moved closer until all were working within fifty yards of him.

The dust cloud swept closer, topped a high spot in the road, and became Kennebeck leading a dozen galloping men. Lew waited until he w' within three hundred yards. Then he crosse his horse and withdrew his rifle from the boot.

The others grouped around him and waited. He glanced quickly around at their faces. He could see fear in them, and doubt, but he could also see unyielding stubbornness.

They would fight for him, he realized suddenly. They would fight even though they were afraid.

Kennebeck hauled his horse to a plunging halt a dozen feet from Lew. His face was livid as he glanced at those surrounding him. His eyes were virulent. But there was something else in those angry eyes. There was an instability that told Lew he had lost what reason remained to him.

Kennebeck would not react, today, like a normal or reasonable man. There would be no restraint in him. He had only one purpose left in life and he wouldn't care how he accomplished it or what he had to do to accomplish it. He wanted to see Lew hanging from the scaffold in Kennebeck. If he had to kill a dozen men to take Lew, he'd kill them without regrets.

Kennebeck stared at him wildly. "I've got you now, you son-of-a-bitch! There's a new scaffold in town and you're going to hang from it!"

Lew didn't answer him because Lew was staring at defeat. He couldn't involve these men around him in what Kennebeck meant to do. If Kennebeck's men started shooting, the men on the ground wouldn't have a chance.

Chavez said: "No! You turn around and go

home, Mister Kennebeck. If you've got a complaint, you send the sheriff after Lew."

Kennebeck didn't seem to have heard. He had not taken his eyes from Lew. Still without looking away from him, he spoke to his men: "Take him! I want him alive!"

There was a sudden shifting of horses. Kennebeck's men moved forward, slowly and inexorably, in a solid line.

The men behind Lew shifted, too, spreading out in order to have more room to shoot.

Lew could have said—"Get Kennebeck first."— and they would have gotten him. But not before several of their number died before the ready guns of Kennebeck's crew.

He hadn't much time to make up his mind and there didn't seem to be much choice. Either he surrendered himself or he let those around him be butchered. And yet . . .

He yelled: "Hold it! Kennebeck wants to see me hang. All right, let *him* take me then! The rest of you stay out of it." He stared up at Kennebeck. "Come on, Kennebeck. This time the law isn't going to do your killing for you. Neither is your crew. You're going to have to do it all by yourself. If you've got the guts for it."

He saw the wildness flare in Kennebeck's eyes. He saw the deep stain that spread from his neck up across his already livid face. He said: "With guns or without. Take your pick, big man. Let` see how good you are at doing your own dirty work."

Kennebeck flung himself from his horse. He stumbled, but recovered and plunged toward Lew. As he did, he unbuckled his gun belt and flung it away from him.

Lew had no time to unbuckle his, only time to snatch out his gun and throw it on the ground. He knew, even before Kennebeck reached him, that he had let himself be pulled into a fight he couldn't win. He was weak from loss of blood and his leg still would not support his weight reliably. He knew he could count on Kennebeck to hurt the wounded leg at every opportunity.

He should have insisted on a showdown with guns. Yet even in this moment of peril, he understood why he had not. He didn't really want to kill Kennebeck, in spite of all the man had done to him. He didn't want to kill Sara's father unless there was no other way.

He side-stepped Kennebeck's first rush, but his leg gave way under the sudden shift of weight and he sprawled against the newly strung fence.

Barbs raked his arm and the side of his neck. He fought to rise as Kennebeck turned, nostrils flared, eyes completely wild. Kennebeck's voice was hoarse. "Anything goes, understand? Anything! I got your old man and I got your brother Jess. Now I'm going to get you!"

He stooped and yanked the steel bar out of a

roll of wire that was lying at his feet. Holding it in both hands, he advanced toward Lew.

Lew crouched slightly, glancing to right and left at the ground on either side. He could afford no stumbles now, no falls. If he faltered, the bar would smash his skull.

Half a dozen feet away, Kennebeck stood, flat-footed, and swung. Lew ducked. But the first swing was a feint to see which way he would move. Kennebeck stopped it in mid-swing and swung a second time, this time in earnest.

There was no way Lew could avoid it short of sprawling flat on the ground. He did and it grazed his back as he fell.

The bar's weight and momentum swung Kennebeck sideways. Lew knew he had no time to get up before it would swing again.

He clawed forward along the ground and threw his weight against Kennebeck's legs. The man toppled, still clinging to the bar. Lew clawed beyond him and struggled to his feet.

His breath ran in and out gustily. He glanced around desperately. He couldn't fight a crowbar with his bare hands. He needed something . . .

A shovel lay nearby. He lunged for it, seized it, and straightened as Kennebeck came charging at him again. The bar swung and Lew dodged back.

He jabbed with the shovel, catching Kennebeck in the forearm. Blood gushed from the ragged gash. This time Kennebeck did not try to stop his swing but continued it, whirling all the way around, putting extra force into the whistling, heavy bar.

It caught Lew squarely on the left thigh with an impact he thought must surely snap the bone. His whole leg went numb and he collapsed like an undercut spruce.

His chest heaving, Kennebeck stood over him, the bar poised for a final, killing blow.

Lew threw the shovel like a javelin. It struck Kennebeck in the throat but it did not stop that last, savage swing. The bar came cutting down.

Lew rolled desperately and it missed his head. But it grazed his shoulder, turning that almost as numb as his leg.

Kennebeck stumbled back, his throat bleeding. The bar lay beside Lew but he could not get up. He was lying on something hard, a rock perhaps, and he shifted to get off of it.

Kennebeck slammed against one of the horses of his men. The animal snorted at the smell of blood and reared.

Lew rolled off the hard object digging into his back. His hand closed on it just as Kennebeck snatched a rifle from his crewman's hands. The man whirled, crouching, blood streaming from throat and forearm, a red and bloody look in his distended eyes. He jacked a cartridge in and flung the gun to his shoulder. He fired.

The bullet struck the bar at Lew's side with

a deafening, clanging sound, then ricocheted away. And Lew realized at the same instant that he was clutching his own gun which he had thrown away only moments before at the start of the fight. The gun was the object that had been digging into him

No time to think. Kennebeck jacked in a second shell and Lew knew he would not miss this time. The bore of the rifle stared blackly at him.

He thumbed back the hammer, half rolling as he did. Without taking time to raise the gun and sight it, he fired.

He continued his roll and came to a sitting position at its end. He raised the gun and fired again.

Kennebeck, already off balance from the first bullet, staggered back against the fence under the impact of the second. He hung there against the tightly strung wire for an instant, then started sliding down. The barbs hooked in his clothes and held him upright though his head lolled forward. The rifle slipped from his nerveless hands and fell to the ground at his feet.

Lew tried to get up, but found that he could not. There was a stinging sensation in his right shoulder. He put up a hand and it came away wet with blood. The bullet that struck the bar must have shattered, he thought, and filled his shoulder with fragments.

Chavez came and helped him up. Lew hung wearily, half on Chavez's supporting arm, half on the top wire of the fence. He looked at the awestruck members of Kennebeck's crew. "Take him home. This fight's finished now."

He thought it would take them forever to load Kennebeck's body, but it couldn't have because when he turned, he could see someone running toward him from the blackened ruins of his house. It was a woman.

He shook off Chavez's arm and began to walk toward her, slowly, slowly, careful of the weight on his numb left leg. He made perhaps a dozen steps before she reached him.

Her face was wet with tears, but there was a wonderful relief in her eyes, and the brave beginnings of a smile upon her mouth.

He said harshly: "I killed him. I killed your father."

"Yes, Lew. I know."

"I said I killed your father. Didn't you hear me?"

"I heard, Lew. But I also saw the fight."

"But . . ."

"Do you want me to hate you for killing him? I can't and I won't. Let his hate die with him." Her chin was trembling and she was very close to hysteria.

He closed his arms tightly around her, feeling her warmth and softness and suddenly very glad he had come home.

The wounds of hate would heal. He stared over her head at the charred buildings down in the yard. He would build a new house just like the old one. Then, perhaps, he could forget.

ABOUT THE AUTHOR

Lewis B. Patten wrote more than ninety Western novels in thirty years, and three of them won Spur Awards from the Western Writers of America, and the author received the Golden Saddleman Award. Indeed, this points up the most remarkable aspect of his work: not that there is so much of it, but that so much of it is so fine. Patten was born in Denver, Colorado, and served in the U.S. Navy, 1933-1937. He was educated at the University of Denver during the war years and became an auditor for the Colorado Department of Revenue during the 1940s. It was in this period that he began contributing significantly to Western pulp magazines, fiction that was from the beginning fresh and unique and revealed Patten's lifelong concern with the sociological and psychological affects of group psychology on the frontier. He became a professional writer at the time of his first novel, *Massacre at White River* (1952). The dominant theme in much of his fiction is the notion of justice, and its opposite, injustice. In his first novel it has to do with exploitation of the Ute Indians, but as he matured as a writer he explored this theme with significant and poignant detail in small towns throughout the early West.

Crimes, such as rape or lynching, are often at the center of his stories. When the values embodied in these small towns are examined closely, they are found to be wanting. Conformity is always easier than taking a stand. Yet, in Patten's view of the American West, there is usually a man or a woman who refuses to conform. Among his finest titles, always a difficult choice, are surely *Death of a Gunfighter* (1968), *A Death in Indian Wells* (1970), and *The Law at Cottonwood* (1978). No less noteworthy are his previous Five Star Westerns, *Tincup in the Storm Country* (1996), *Trail to Vicksburg* (1997), *Death Rides the Denver Stage* (1999), *The Woman at Ox-Yoke* (2000), and *Ride the Red Trail* (2001).

Books are produced in the United States using U.S.-based materials

Books are printed using a revolutionary new process called THINK tech™ that lowers energy usage by 70% and increases overall quality

Books are durable and flexible because of smythe-sewing

Paper is sourced using environmentally responsible foresting methods and the paper is acid-free

Center Point Large Print
600 Brooks Road / PO Box 1
Thorndike, ME 04986-0001 USA

(207) 568-3717

US & Canada:
1 800 929-9108
www.centerpointlargeprint.com